A BODYGUARDS BOOK

J.V. SPEYER

For Sophia

Chapter One

Eric wrinkled his nose and looked over his desk. His last two partners had called him a neat freak, and his need for tidiness might have had something to do with the reasons they'd broken up. (Eric preferred to think it had more to do with both men having an inability to put the cap back on the toothpaste or rinse a damn dish before putting it into the dishwasher, but everyone had their own side to a story.)

Looking over his desk now, he had to admit their arguments might have held weight.

A piece of paper—a memo from the dean from the looks of it, the guy never would just email his message blasts like an environmentally conscious citizen should—had drifted from his in-box when he opened the door. He carefully put it back in the stack, making sure it didn't stick out any more or less than the other pieces of paper.

Okay, his exes' arguments had a lot of merit. Eric refused to be shamed.

He set his coffee cup down (on a coaster, where it couldn't disturb anything or leave a mark) and checked his messages. He always needed extra coffee after teaching the foundational courses. He tried to remember cardinal virtues like patience. Everyone started somewhere, and while these underclassmen might not have a strong aptitude for whichever subject he was teaching at the moment, they'd at least made the decision to be here. They wanted to be part of the solution.

At least these students were trying, unlike so much of the rest of the world.

He scrolled through his messages, desperately hoping something would catch his eye and wake him up. He kept hoping to see news from *Environmental Research Quarterly* about the paper he'd submitted regarding solar-powered desalinization and purification plants. He didn't think they'd have a reason to bounce the research. He knew his business, and he even had hard data to back it up, thanks to his stepfather's open mind and foresight. Still, the wheels of academia turned slowly, and at least he hadn't found a rejection letter today.

So far, nothing in his in-box related to him specifically. At best, he had "informational" emails sent out to groups of people. In five years on the faculty, he hadn't once opted to participate on the department softball team. That wasn't going to change this year, even with another formulaic email exhorting him to JOIN IN THE FUN! Every once in a while, he found an automated message about a student having difficulties, but those didn't require action on his part. He filed them away for later reference, if needed, and sighed. He'd better wake up before his one o'clock environmental law class. Environmental law was one of his favorite classes to teach, but if he wasn't on his game, it would be drier than bone.

Three Nigerian princes also desperately wanted to give him money. He always got a chuckle out of that one.

His door was open, but someone knocked on it anyway. Arthur Sellers, Dean of the Faculty of Arts and Sciences, cleared his throat and walked in without waiting. A shorter man, Black and in clerical garb with a white cap on his head, followed. Eric recognized the university's still-new Islamic chaplain. He'd met Dr. Omar a few times, although Eric's experience with formalized religion of any sort made him keep his distance.

"Dr. Alawi?" Sellers tugged at his collar. His tie was too tight, as usual, and it made him look like he was being strangled. Eric could see the ligature mark. "You remember Dr. Omar."

Eric stood and bowed his head. Omar did the same. Omar seemed like a decent man, and probably made a perfectly fine chaplain.

"Of course. How can I help you?" Eric plastered a bland smile on his face. The last time these two had come to see him in tandem, it was because a graduate student from the Chemistry department was stuck at the airport due to a travel ban. Eric didn't think he had time before his next class to go all the way up to Logan and translate, but he'd find a way if he had to. He'd done it before.

Omar stepped forward, his face grave. "I'm afraid we're here for you, Dr. Alawi. We're here to be the bearers of bad news. Your sister and brother-in-law were killed last night in a drunk driving accident."

Eric stared. Both of his guests probably expected a more extreme reaction, but Eric couldn't think for the life of him who they might be talking about. "I'm sorry. Both of my parents married more than once. I'm going to have to ask you to narrow it down."

"Of course." Sellers closed the door gently and turned around. "The attorney I spoke with said it was your older sister, Selene. The attorney said he didn't have contact information for you, but she

4

told him where you worked. She lived in Weston, it seems?"

Eric couldn't breathe for a second. Selene had been living in Weston? To be sure, Eric didn't get out to explore the suburbs all that often, but he at least knew where Weston *was*. The idea of one of his childhood nemeses living only fifteen miles from him made his blood run cold. "I. I see." He swallowed. "And how long has she been living in Weston?"

"I couldn't say." Omar exchanged glances with Sellers. "I take it you didn't see each other often."

"I haven't seen her since I was . . . oh, twelve, maybe." Eric took a deep breath and tried to settle his thoughts. Selene had been living less than thirty miles away, and Eric hadn't known. It was as good a metaphor as any for his family relationships, he guessed. "I suppose I won't . . ." He cut himself off. His feelings weren't at issue here, and he didn't need to go displaying them for his colleagues. "Has our father been notified?"

"I would assume so. We were notified because your sister's attorneys called us. I couldn't speak to the rest of the notification chain." Sellers narrowed his eyes, a little suspiciously. "You're going to need to go down to Mass General."

5

"And what, claim the bodies?" Eric glanced at his desk, his calendar, his laptop. "I have classes to teach." He closed his eyes, aware of the impression he was giving. "I'm sorry. I know that seems callous to you. It's just—it's been well over a decade since I've seen her. I don't even know her husband's name. Can't the consulate send someone?"

He clamped his lips together. Throwing phrases around like *can't the consulate send someone* was dangerous. Perhaps the news was having more of an effect than he thought.

Omar stayed still for a few seconds. Then a light seemed to dawn behind his dark eyes. "Dr. Alawi, you don't need to go down to Mass General to retrieve their bodies. Arrangements have already been made, as I understand it. The attorneys can explain everything when you see them. But your sister left behind a child."

No other sound penetrated Eric's mind, not even the ancient copier clunking away in front of his office. "A child."

Omar grabbed Eric's sport coat from the back of the door as Sellers packed up Eric's laptop.

"I'll get someone else to cover your classes for you," Sellers explained as Omar helped him into his jacket. "Right now, you have other things to think about. There are people who need you." He

6

patted Eric on the back. "Go on. Call an Uber or something. I'll hold down the fort here." His sonorous, ancient Boston-brahmin accent washed over Eric while he shuffled over to the door.

Omar wound up calling for a Lyft, which turned out to be driven by one of Eric's graduate students. Eric managed to recover enough of his senses to thank him and leave him a generous tip, but he couldn't remember one minute of the drive from Harvard down to the warren-like complex by the banks of the Charles that was Mass General.

A volunteer brought them to the pediatric ward, brightly painted with sunny murals. Somewhere an alarm went off, sending people wearing scrubs running.

The volunteer kept moving toward the appropriate room unfazed. "You understand, of course, why there are police outside the door. We've managed to keep the story out of the media so far, but that can only last so long." He smiled a brittle smile. "People like to know these things, Your Highness."

Omar did a double take, and Eric cringed.

"Please. Dr. Alawi will be just fine. Royal titles don't mean much in a country without a king." Eric forced a little smile. It seemed more appropriate than running away and changing his name again.

Eric's stomach roiled again as he saw the police officers outside the room. "Are you sure everyone is reading this right?"

"The lawyers will explain everything." The volunteer bowed slightly and scurried off.

Omar leaned in. "The school didn't tell me you're royalty."

"I didn't tell them." Eric silently cursed the volunteer and his loose lips. "Thank you for coming down here with me. Do you want to come in, or would you rather avoid it?"

Omar took a deep breath. "I'll come with you." A tiny smile made the edges of his mouth twitch. "I don't get the impression you're all that familiar with how to handle small children. I have four of my own. If nothing else, I may be able to help you in that way."

"You've already helped more than I can say." Eric made himself smile. Omar had been more helpful than Eric could have imagined a chaplain would be. And Eric had no experience at all with small children, so anything would help.

He steeled himself and pushed his way into the room. He didn't know exactly what he expected to find. He had little experience with hospitals—mostly emergency situations, when he needed to translate for grieving or injured people. Still, he had no idea what Selene's child would look like. If they were in an open ward, he wouldn't know which one he was supposed to visit. He'd embarrass everyone, especially himself, and probably traumatize the poor little one even worse.

A little girl, maybe four years old, sat up in a beige hospital johnny. Her hair was an utter mess, and her eyes were red and swollen. "I don't wanna go live with a guy!" she screamed. "I wanna live with you!"

Two men in suits stood on the far side of the room, their pupils smaller than some purely theoretical particles. They looked ready to bolt at the next thing that went wrong.

On the end of the little girl's bed sat an exhausted-looking man, probably in his midthirties, with the most amazing arms Eric had ever seen. Sandy-brown hair, clipped short but not shaved, crowned a face that could have graced the cover of a thousand magazines. He wore jeans and a plain white T-shirt, both of which would look much better on the floor.

Eric kicked himself mentally. He wasn't here to ogle some man. He was here to help this child. "Hello. I'm Eric Alawi. I was told to come here . . ."

The man on the bed jumped up. His reactions were those of a soldier, even if his clothes were pure James Dean Americana. "This guy?" He jerked his thumb at Eric as he faced the men in suits.

9

"This guy? They left this beautiful girl to some weirdo in a suit instead of to her uncle, who she knows and loves?" He advanced on the lawyers with his hand in a fist. Eric half expected to see him pull a gun.

"Like hell am I going to let her go with some stranger who couldn't even be bothered to get to know her. Or show up to the goddamned wedding."

Eric pressed his lips together hard enough to hurt. "Perhaps this is a discussion better had in the hallway and not in front of an already distressed child?"

The angry man turned bright red and wheeled on the men in suits again. "Would you listen to him? He's so stuck-up, he's looking down at the Hancock Tower!" He threw his hands up. "Fine. Whatever. Ada, you stay in bed, okay, sweetheart?"

"Okay, Uncle Dan." She sniffed and rubbed at her eyes.

Wonderful. At least the tiny ball of rage had a name.

Eric led the probable lawyers and Uncle Dan out into the hall. Omar stayed in the child's room, for reasons Eric didn't understand but were probably important.

10

He took a deep breath. "Very well. Since I am clearly the one with the least information, can someone please fill me in on what is happening and who you might be?" He looked Uncle Dan up and down.

"I'm that kid's uncle. I'm her freaking world right now, and I'm not letting you take her."

One of the lawyers cleared his throat. This one looked rich, in an understated way. He was probably the partner in charge of the case. "Mr. Marshall, I'm afraid there isn't any 'let' involved here. Each of your siblings chose Dr. Adler—"

"Alawi." Eric held up a hand. "I don't use my father's name." He didn't feel compelled to explain more than that.

"You see? He might technically be related, but he skipped out on the wedding, he doesn't use the name, and he sounds like some snot from a bad Jane Austen flick. He can't take that kid. He'd probably leave her with the butler and go drink tea or something." Dan stepped closer to Eric, bristling.

Eric frowned at Dan. He shouldn't care what the man thought of him, but his attitude toward Eric's relationship with his family pissed him off. "First of all, 'Uncle Dan,' I don't know you. I don't care to know you at this point, but you're making an awful lot of assumptions about me. I don't use my father's name because paparazzi do make it

11

ever so hard for the undergraduates to do their thing." He tried to keep the contempt from his voice. He failed miserably, but he put the effort in.

"And given that I wasn't invited to the wedding, nor informed of Selene's engagement, nor informed that she was living so close to me, I think I can be excused for my absence. Seeing as how I was unwelcome, and all. I haven't seen Selene since I was twelve, nor anyone on that side of the family since I was fifteen and outed. So spare me your outrage, or find someone who gives a damn."

Dan took a step back. His face went from rage-red to a more typical pink. "Then why would they leave Ada to you instead of me? I'm close to her. She actually likes me."

The partner stepped between them. Eric appreciated the gesture. It made it easier to hide the metaphorical stab wound.

"If I may. I did help to draw up the documents involved. Mr. Marshall, your brother and sister-in-law cared very deeply for you. They appointed you the executor of their estate and the trustee of Ada's trust fund. They acknowledged just how much Ada loves you. But Mr.—er, Dr. Alawi isn't just a scholar of some renown. He's a member of the Corvian royal family and his grandfather owns half the oil in the Middle East."

12

"Can we not?" Eric turned away in disgust. "If I wanted that to be part of my life, I'd go to one of those countries and live there." He left out the part where it wasn't an option for him. Somehow, it didn't seem helpful.

"I notice you don't turn down the money though." Dan smirked at him, as if he knew the first thing about where Eric's money came from.

"*Nevertheless.*" The lawyer scowled at them both.

Eric hadn't felt so small since he was a schoolboy back in . . . oh, which boarding school had it been?

"His experience with staying out of the limelight and living his own life had become something Mrs. Marshall was deeply concerned with by the time she and your brother got married. Also, I believe she had concerns about some other members of her family. Dr. Alawi has the means, both diplomatic and financial, to resist them better than you do."

"I work for a goddamn security contractor!"

The attorney cleared his throat and turned the full force of his ire onto Dan. "And yet one of you seems to be committed to maintaining a low profile while one of you is shouting loud enough to be heard on Beacon Hill."

13

"But she's never even met him!" Dan slapped his hand against the wall, drawing the eyes of several nurses.

"I have to agree with Mr. Marshall." Eric stepped away from Dan. "His anger notwithstanding, it's simply absurd to think the child is going to adapt well to moving in with a stranger so soon after such a terrible loss."

"You didn't even know them." Dan scoffed and turned away.

"I don't have to. I don't even have to like them. The last time I saw Selene she pushed me down the stairs at a state function back in Corvia, for no reason other than her own entertainment. It was all caught on camera, and the tabloids had fun with it for weeks after. That doesn't mean I don't know perfectly well how terrible the loss of a parent feels. I can empathize with Ada."

Dan might be beautiful, but he was a terrible person. Eric genuinely hoped he was straight, so they never accidentally ran into each other under better circumstances.

Eric pulled himself in. He shouldn't let himself think that way. Dan had, apparently, just lost his brother. He'd also evidently been closer to his brother than Eric had ever been with any of his.

"She should stay with him," he told the lawyer.

14

The lawyer looked down. "As much as I'd like to accommodate you, the terms of your sister's will are ironclad. If you refuse to take custody of Ada, I'm obligated to disclose the name you're living under and your parentage to local media. She mentioned something about an old home movie as well."

Eric cursed out loud this time. Leave it to Selene to reach out from a drawer in the medical examiner's office to humiliate him anew. "Why would she do that?"

"She felt strongly about guaranteeing the child her privacy." The lawyer raised his eyebrow. "She wanted to make sure you would too."

Chapter Two

Dan counted to ten. He knew he didn't have a leg to stand on. He could spend ten years in court, but he wasn't going to get custody of Ada. Ben had apparently agreed with Selene on giving Ada to this Eric guy for whatever reason, even if it was the dumbest thing ever. Dan could contest it, but he couldn't afford decent lawyers, and even he knew going against a parent's final wishes for their child would be an exercise in futility. A smart soldier didn't fight a battle he'd already lost.

"You don't even want her." Okay, so maybe Dan hadn't ever been the smartest soldier in the unit. He was still a better guardian for Ada than this jerk.

Eric—*Doctor* Eric, who couldn't even be bothered to use his family's last name—bowed his head. For a moment, he looked profoundly old. Then he lifted his head again, squared his shoulders, and met Dan's eyes. "Up until an hour ago, I didn't know she existed. There's no want or don't want; it's about what's best for the child. I'm not convinced living with me is best for her. And I am trying very hard not to believe your volatile temper indicates that you are also not in the child's best interests." He hesitated and looked away.

"I have no interest in keeping the child from you. I can see you were close with your brother, and I'm sorry for your loss. The girl has had enough of a heartbreak without some stranger bursting in and cutting her off from everything familiar. The last thing I want is to contribute to her trauma—more than Selene's already forced me to, of course."

Dan pressed his lips together. Everything Eric was saying was true. Dan was lashing out, in part because of his grief. If everything Eric was saying was true, he must be reeling from shock. It didn't change anything, but Dan could probably stand to be a little nicer.

"I'm sorry. I am upset, but you didn't plan this." He took a deep breath. "No one did. I'm sure even Selene thought all this was a long shot." He cleared his throat. "Who's your friend in there?"

"He's a chaplain from the university." Eric's mouth twisted, and suddenly, he looked almost kissable. With his full lips, loose, dark curls, and bright eyes, Eric just might have been the hottest guy to grace Boston's streets in years.

18

Dan pushed the thought away. This wasn't the time for anything like that, and certainly not with any of Selene's snotty relatives. "You brought the chaplain with you?" All he needed was for his brand-new nemesis to start barfing some religious drivel at the kids.

"I was a little stunned. He volunteered. Again, until an hour ago, I had no idea I had family in the area." He shook his head, like he was clearing it. "Right. Time for rumination later." He turned to the head lawyer—Fred, if Dan remembered correctly. "I assume Ada is medically cleared to leave?"

"She is. You'll want her to come and live in your home, I assume?" Fred pulled out his phone, looking at Eric.

"I'm afraid it isn't childproofed, but we'll have to make do." Eric rubbed at his handsome face. "Dan, I hate to ask you to do anything at a time like this, but I don't know who else to ask. I assume you have a key to your brother's home?"

Dan nodded. He had a key, all right. He had no idea what the hell a guy like Eric would want with it. "You bet. Why?"

"Because my house doesn't have a child-appropriate bed. Or toys. I'll pay for a van and I'll happily pay students to help lift and carry, but I don't know where the house is or what Ada will

19

want." He stuffed his hands into his pockets. "This is something I cannot do."

Dan fought back a furious retort. He knew Eric wasn't being some snob by asking Dan to take care of this. He was being smart and understanding his limits. Dan needed to put his grief and anger aside until he could direct it correctly.

"Yeah. Yeah, sorry." He ran his hand through his hair and blew out a sigh. "I can do that, just tell me where to take the stuff."

Eric's shoulders lost a little bit of their tightness. He pulled out his phone and sent a couple of messages. "Thank you. I have some students on their way to help—is two enough?"

"Yeah, sure." Must be nice to be able to commandeer labor just like that. Dan scowled and turned to the lawyer. "I'm going to go tell Ada what's going on. You want to give Dr. Eric here a crash course in the care and feeding of a four-year-old or whatever?" He took off toward Ada's room before he realized he still had no idea where Eric lived.

His brother wouldn't have stormed off like that. Ben would have taken the time to get the guy's address. Ben would have become Eric's best friend, within minutes. He pulled out his phone, now that he was on the verge of reentering his niece's room,

20

and dialed Ben's number. He'd have some advice on how to patch things up.

The call went straight to voice mail. *Hi, this is Ben. I can't get to the phone right now—*

Dan hung up with a strangled scream. *Goddamn it. Damn it all.*

He took a few deep breaths. All of this was overwhelming, and he felt like he couldn't do it. Just because he felt like he couldn't do it didn't make it so. Eric might be a stuck-up prick, but he definitely had a cooler head on his shoulders and at least seemed to be thinking about what Ada needed. Dan needed to do the same thing, damn it.

He called his boss, Levi, instead.

Levi picked up right away, even though it was pretty damn early in Colorado. "Hey, Dan. How's it going in the land of dirty water, buddy?"

Dan let his sigh convey everything he couldn't say with words. "It's . . . it's a lot. It turns out Ben and Selene left the kid to her brother. A guy I've never met. A guy *the kid* has never met. Apparently, Selene didn't invite this guy to the wedding. He doesn't even use the family name, but she wants him to have Ada over me?"

Levi winced. "Ouch. That sucks, bro. What's his name?"

Dan perked up, just a little bit. Levi might be able to find some dirt to get the kid away from Eric. "Eric Alawi. Also Eric Adler."

"Two names, huh? Pretty sneaky." Eric heard Levi's fingers dance over the keyboard. "Wait—would that be the royal family of Corvia, Adler?"

"That's the one. Selene pissed the fam off when she married some American scumbag like Ben." Dan chuckled, remembering everything Ben had gone through when the courtship was announced. It all seemed so petty now. "Her dad was *pissed*."

Levi whistled. "Looks like the brother's more or less a ghost. I've got a bunch of academic papers, he's a bit of a recluse, got his PhD at a young age from Yale—I can't see any argument against him. Seems to stay out of the limelight, at least." Levi paused. "Do you get a weird vibe from him?"

Dan considered. Levi wasn't asking him as a grieving brother, but as a professional and a former Ranger. "I don't have the distance to make that assessment. I hate him too much. He's saying all the right things, but I just ..." The Army hadn't included training on how to verbalize the tangle of complicated feelings in his belly at the moment.

"You don't have to figure it out right now. You're on leave for the moment." Levi's voice was kind. "Focus on that little girl."

"I'm trying, Levi. There's just this slim pretentious roadblock in the way."

Levi chuckled. "I've never seen a roadblock a Ranger couldn't get over. Check in with me tonight, would you?"

"Will do." Dan hung up.

He rubbed at his face. He didn't need to figure everything out today. All he needed to do was to get Ada's things together. She was the most important part of all this.

A big ancient-looking van rattled up to the curb. The side of the van proclaimed it to belong to the Harvard Archaeology Department, which explained why it looked like a relic. The people inside were not relics. The younger one, with red hair in the passenger seat, might have been too young to go to Basic. "Are you Dan Marshall?" the kid asked, in a voice that confirmed puberty wasn't done with him yet.

I'm not getting in that thing.

Dan pushed his resentment to the side. It was for his niece. "Yeah. Did Doc Eric send you?"

The redheaded kid paled, but the driver just nodded. He looked older, and like he hadn't slept in at least twenty-four hours. "Yeah, he called us. Hop in."

Dan obeyed, against his better judgment. If the floor on this old death trap didn't fall out from under them, he'd consider it a miracle. "I'd have thought Harvard could afford a better ride, given that they own all of Cambridge and Allston."

"Right?" The driver snickered as Dan buckled into the passenger seat. "Here, tell the GPS where we're going. Yeah, whatever they're spending all that cash on, it doesn't trickle down. I'm Adrian, I'm Eric's graduate assistant. This is Bill, he's a freshman and he's getting paid beer money."

Dan plugged Ben's address into the GPS. He wasn't going to make a fuss about freshmen drinking beer. He'd deployed to his first war zone well before Bill's age, and he'd damn well had a beer before leaving. "Awesome. Um, did he tell you what we were doing?"

"No. Just that it was an emergency. He's usually the first one there for us, so I sure wasn't going to say no." Adrian pulled carefully out onto Storrow. "Are you a boyfriend or what?"

"What? No." Dan fought against an image of himself kissing that pretentious accent right out of Eric. "My brother was married to his sister. They were killed last night in a DUI."

24

"Oh my God." Adrian widened his eyes. "I'm so sorry for your loss." He waited a beat. "I didn't even know Eric had a sister."

"Yeah, well. I guess there's some drama there. Too late to fix it now." Dan massaged his temples. "We've just got to go in—they had a kid, Eric got custody." He took a breath. How were Eric and his chaplain buddy dealing with Ada? And how was Ada handling the chaplain and the strange uncle? "Our sibs left her to him for whatever reason, so we've got to get things like her clothes and toys and whatever."

Adrian scoffed. "Yeah, he definitely doesn't have anything like that in his house. Plenty of books though." He grimaced. "What the hell is Eric going to do with a kid? One of the admins asked him to hold her baby, and I thought he was going to die of fright."

"That's not a good sign." Dan frowned and looked out the window. "Hopefully, he'll figure it out, I guess." He put his arm across his abdomen as though it could settle the way his stomach turned.

It didn't take them long to pack up Ada's things and get them in the van. The neighbors didn't seem to notice anything going on, or if they did, they didn't say anything. Dan moved through the process in a haze of grief. If he could concentrate on just putting one foot in front of the other, he could probably get through this. Probably.

He couldn't make himself go into his brother's space—not his home office and not the bedroom. Sometime later, in a few weeks, he'd have to clear the place out. He'd have to donate Ben's clothes, and he'd have to sort out what to keep and what to save of the rest of his estate. Same with Selene's things. Today, he couldn't bring himself to do it. These two college kids, with their artistically shabby clothes that probably cost more than a whole month's pay, wouldn't be there. They couldn't possibly understand.

Adrian knew where Eric lived, as it turned out. Dan didn't mind being spared the embarrassment of having to find a way to ask. Eric's place was walking distance to Harvard Square, because of course it was. Why wouldn't an actual prince have some kind of palatial estate within walking distance of America's snootiest college?

Only in Cambridge did a quarter of an acre count as a palatial estate, but Dan's dad had worked on a lot of these old homes. He knew damn well what this mansion was worth.

The place had a tall stockade fence around it, with a gate that required a pass and a code to get in. The professional in Dan admired Eric's

26

foresight, but the Southie-born Bostonian just turned up his nose. *What a snob.* Adrian had both the pass and the code, so the van got in with no problem. A dark-haired woman let them into the house, although she gave Dan and Bill a baleful look.

There was a cat, a rough-looking gray-striped thing with one eye. It sat near the woman's feet and hissed at Dan.

"He says he doesn't care which room they pick for the poor child," the woman told Adrian, in a voice with a heavy accent. Dan would have to guess she came from somewhere in the Gulf, just from her accent, although she dressed like any other American. "He says to ask the uncle."

All eyes swiveled to land on Dan. "How should I know?" he sputtered. "I've never even been here before!" He swallowed. "Okay, okay. Um, let's . . . go see which rooms are available." He followed Adrian up the stairs, an armload of kid gear in his arms.

He picked a bedroom for Ada mostly based on distance from the master. Eric apparently had plenty of bedrooms to spare. There was a whole third level with even more bedrooms, but Dan didn't think sticking Ada on the third level would be the way to go. Why did a single guy need so many bedrooms, anyway? He shook his head and got to work setting up the room in a way that made it look less like a museum.

Eric arrived at the house not long afterward. It wasn't hard to tell when he got home. A loud *ping* split the air, and Ada's screams followed.

"I don't want to live here!" Her howls were shrill enough to pierce glass. "It's weird!"

Dan bowed his head. He didn't want her to live here either. He put down the tools the strange foreign woman had found and went to see what the problem was.

Eric had led Ada into the kitchen, which was spotless and completely unprepared for the sudden appearance of a four-year-old. He grabbed her a glass of water—because giving a child that age something breakable was such a grand idea—and dropped to his knees in front of her. "I know it's weird, Ada. It's certainly very different from what you're used to. Having a child living here will be different from what I'm used to, too." He held the glass to Ada's lips.

Against everything Dan thought possible, Ada let Eric help her drink. "But it's weird," she said again in a softer tone. "I want my mommy."

Eric just nodded, giving no sign that talking to such a small child was any different than talking to any of his colleagues at the school. "Did you know my mother also died in a car accident?"

28

Ada narrowed her eyes at him. "Really? You're just saying it."

"No, it's true. I was sixteen years old at the time, so I was bigger than you are now. But she did, and I miss her very much. It's okay to miss your mom, and it's okay to be mad about how much things are changing. No one here will be upset with you about that."

Ada bit her lip. "But you can't make it go back."

"No. I would if I could."

The woman who'd let them in stepped forward and rattled off a stream of Arabic too fast for Dan to follow. He spoke a little, just enough to get by, but this was beyond him.

Eric answered her in the same language and gave her a thin fleeting smile. The woman left again, giving Dan another suspicious glare.

"Who's the lady?" Ada tilted her head to the side, although the glint of suspicion never quite left her eyes.

"That's Hadiya. She lives here and helps me take care of the house and with the cooking. She's going to go out and get some things for you, so you don't end up hungry. She had children of her own, so she knows what you'll need better than I do." Eric never took his eyes away from hers. He didn't talk down to her either.

Dan didn't want to give Eric the slightest bit of credit, but he had to admit Eric might not suck at this after all.

"I don't want you to make Uncle Dan go away." Ada turned to Dan and grabbed his hand. "Uncle Dan, please don't go."

Eric's jaw tightened, just a little, but he looked up at Dan. "Your uncle is welcome to stay as long as he likes or as long as you need him to. We both want what's best for you."

Dan's mouth went dry. He thought back to his apartment in Denver and how much he didn't want to have to be around a guy like Eric. He looked down into Ada's eyes.

"Yeah. Whatever you need, Ada."

Chapter Three

Eric tried to hold the hairbrush, instead of throwing it across the room the way Ada had. He was an adult. He didn't need to resort to a child's techniques for coping. And how hard could it be to comb a child's hair, anyway? It was supposed to be soothing. All the child development sites he'd read during her nap suggested it.

Dan snatched the brush out of his hand. "What are you trying to do, snatch the hair off her head? This isn't *Drag Race.* She's a child. What the hell kind of a grown-ass man doesn't know how to comb a kid's hair?" He pulled Ada away and took to the task himself.

Hadiya gave Dan a look of undisguised loathing. "People who aren't exposed to children can't be expected to miraculously know how to care for them, *soldier.*" She sniffed and moved away from Dan, closer to Eric. Then she switched

31

languages. "Is it absolutely necessary for him to stay here?"

Eric heaved a sigh. "He's the only family the child has. I hardly count—I'm a stranger. I'm sure he'll leave once she's settled in. You're welcome to move into my suite if it makes you more comfortable, or I can put a few more locks on the door to your room. Whatever you need to feel comfortable."

She glared at Dan again. "I don't like him. He isn't safe for you. He doesn't respect you."

"No." Eric shrugged. "But neither does anyone else in my family. Why would he be any different? He's only here temporarily, Hadiya. Let's just make the best of a bad situation."

Hadiya sniffed and stormed over to the cooking area of the kitchen.

"How do you go through life without being 'exposed to children'?" Dan rolled his eyes and shook his head. "Even Ada knows how to deal with babies. And she's four."

Ada stuck her tongue out at Eric.

"My parents separated when I was two. I was probably three when I was sent off to boarding school. While that's young by most standards, it is what it is." Eric kept his back straight. He had nothing to be ashamed of. "I'm not aware of any educational institution that accepts infants

32

however. Perhaps I can offer you something to drink?"

Dan scoffed and focused on the task before him. Eric decided he didn't care. He was more interested in Ada anyway. While Eric's intent had been to soothe her, her long red hair had become a tangled mess through the course of the afternoon and did need attention.

His phone rang, and he pulled it from his pocket. He didn't get a lot of calls, and he was surprised to find his brother's name on the screen. He rarely heard from his father's side of the family at all. Under the circumstances though, he supposed he should have expected it.

"Good evening, Andreas." He didn't try to keep the fatigue from his voice. He spoke English, for Dan and Ada's benefit.

Ada paled at the name. Eric hadn't expected that. Someone with a degree in child psychology should probably look into what had caused a reaction like that, but Eric was beyond ill-equipped to do so. Dan narrowed his eyes at her and at Eric, but said nothing.

"Eric, brother." Andreas' voice had a layer of warmth over it but underneath was the same coldness Eric remembered. The warmth was like a blanket, hiding something ugly underneath. "I

33

know you've heard the news. I've spoken with Selene's attorney. How are you holding up?"

Eric sat down at the breakfast bar, as far from his reluctant guests as he could get. "As well as can be expected. Everything is such a shock, but I'm sure you can imagine why."

"Oh, most certainly. Although you and Selene were keeping secrets, you sly devils. I had no idea you were so close, for her to be giving you guardianship of her daughter. I spoke to her only a few days ago, and she didn't mention seeing you at all."

Eric glanced back over at the Marshalls. They looked like a perfect little family, standing near the table with the elder grooming the younger. They needed nothing else, certainly not some strange foreign man interfering. Dan glanced back over at Eric but didn't say anything.

"Believe me, Andreas. It was as much of a surprise to me as it was to you. I had no idea she'd gotten married, never mind had a child or lived in the same area as I do."

Andreas chuckled softly. "You must have been living under a rock, Eric. It was in all the tabloids. But then again, I suppose you never did make much of an effort to keep up with the latest news." He sniffed. "Fortunately, your standoffishness works in everyone's favor this

34

time. Since the child is a stranger to you and can be of little interest, all things considered, you won't have any problem signing her guardianship over to me."

Eric laughed and covered his mouth with his hand. He hadn't meant to mock Andreas. Surely, Andreas was grieving just as much as Dan was. He might be an absolute shit human, but he was still a human and deserved to grieve in peace.

"Did you just laugh at me?" The little growl in his voice proved the real Andreas was still there, underneath everything.

"I apologize. It's just that Selene's brother-in-law said something similar."

"I am nothing like those apes!" Andreas bellowed his rage directly into Eric's ear, almost making him drop the phone. "You can't honestly believe I'd let an insult like that lie, do you?"

Eric gripped the phone a little tighter. He was a grown man now, not a scared, skinny child. He took the precaution of switching to German before responding, so he didn't offend his guests. "It's not intended as an insult, Andreas. It's simply an observation. You both had the same thought, which isn't necessarily incorrect. Unfortunately for everyone, Selene's will was specific. I can't pass custody of the girl off to you or to the Marshalls. There are dire consequences to me in her will if I do. I certainly think she'd be better off with Dan Marshall—"

"She would not. She's a member of the Corvian royal family, even if she is half-baboon, and she needs to be raised to understand her place in the world. The brat is third in line to the throne itself."

Eric glanced at Ada, whose hair had not yet submitted to the rule of the comb. He tried to picture her undergoing the same rigorous protocol training he'd been forced to suffer through. Perhaps this was why Selene had done what she'd done.

"Nevertheless, Andreas, I can't give the child over to you. Besides, her father's family has the right to see her, know her, and spend time with her."

"Selene made an impetuous decision in a heated and rebellious moment. She never quite forgave father for your existence, or for the existence of the others. If she'd been in her right mind, she'd never have sullied the bloodline with the mongrelized blood of some carpenter in America."

Eric kept his voice neutral and calm. He wasn't going to get anywhere by venting his own anger, and it would only make things worse in the house if the kid or Dan knew what Andreas was

36

saying. "I'm not sure what Ben did for a living, but from what I can see, he loved Selene and Ada beyond words or reason. The family was close-knit and stable, and while I've only met one of Ben's family members, I can say they loved and fiercely defended each other. Even I know that's an important example to put in front of children of any class.

"I know you're grieving, Andreas, and I agree that I'm probably the least qualified person to have custody of this child. That said, I cannot surrender her to you. I hope we can speak again when you're feeling better because I do want her to have some contact with her mother's side of the family too."

"We'll speak about this tomorrow. I'm already in the United States. I'm in Washington for trade talks. It shouldn't take me long to reach Boston." Andreas hung up.

Eric thought he was doing a good job of hiding his reaction, but it had been a long time since he'd had to do anything of the sort.

Dan got up, dropping the brush onto the kitchen island. "Ada, I think it's time for you to hit the sack, what do you think?"

Ada still looked pale, but she sidled up to Eric and leaned against him for a second. "Thank you for not making me live with Uncle Andreas," she whispered, and trotted after Dan.

Well, that was interesting.

Hadiya had already made some tea. She slipped out of the room by the time Dan made it back downstairs. He looked down at the two mugs of tea and then back at Eric. "She didn't drug this, did she?"

Eric rolled his eyes. "Please don't insult my friend and housekeeper. She thinks you're more likely to drug her."

"I know." He tugged at his collar and cleared his throat. "I don't speak it well, but I know enough to know when I'm in trouble. Ranger." He indicated himself, a sheepish half grin on his face.

"Ah." Eric was only vaguely aware of what a Ranger might be, but he didn't want Dan to explain so he just nodded.

Dan sat down and wrapped his hands around a mug. "So. That was your brother."

"I suppose. I have several." Eric closed his eyes. "Apologies. It was a difficult call. He and Selene were close, you see."

"Not so much." Dan took a deep breath. "I understand you weren't ever close to her. I got the chance to know her, you know, as an adult. She didn't have a lot of good things to say about her family." He toyed with the mug handle. "She said she and Andreas used to be close, but as she got older, she realized a lot of that royal scene was pretty toxic. He kind of disgusted her by the end." He rubbed the back of his neck. "I guess what I'm saying is, you might remember them as being two peas in a pod, but she'd never have even thought about letting that dude have custody of the kid."

Eric didn't need Dan to tell him that part. They wouldn't be having this discussion if it had been any other way. He bit his tongue. Dan was trying to be helpful. Eric needed to let him. "Thank you. It's good to have a perspective on her outside of the way I knew her. She had a lot of resentment toward me because of my mother, and that affected how we viewed each other for the rest of her life." He took a deep breath. "Ada seemed perturbed by the possibility of Andreas coming to the house."

Dan screwed up his face. "You picked up on that too, huh? Yeah, I'm not sure what's up with that. She didn't say anything when we were upstairs, only that she didn't want to live with him. She's still not thrilled about living with you, but it's a thousand times better than living with that ass." He blushed. "Sorry. I shouldn't trash your brother like that."

Eric waved a hand. "Trash away. I clearly don't mind." He managed a little smile. "The relationship you have with Ben is special. So many people would kill for it. So many of us would cheerfully sacrifice a limb to have that kind of affection and closeness with a sibling."

Dan ducked his head and looked away. "Yeah . . . about that."

"Sorry. I shouldn't have brought it up." That was Eric—always sticking his foot in his mouth.

"No. Not what I meant. It is special, and I miss him like burning. But, um. There's a bigger issue here. I'm concerned that Ada reacted that strongly to the idea of being around Andreas."

Eric pursed his lips and gave careful consideration to his words. "If I'm being honest, it's a perfectly natural response to being around Andreas. But the nature of this situation, and Selene's choices, makes me suspect Ada hasn't spent enough time around Andreas to be quite so afraid of him."

"Except she *is* this afraid of him." Dan gripped his mug tighter.

"Precisely." Eric sighed again. "I don't know if I can keep him away from the house without risking an international incident. I am concerned however."

"I'm worried about her safety. Especially with Andreas being already in country." He scratched the back of his head. "I know I'm not in the greatest mental state right now, but I've been

40

doing this kind of thing for a long time. I'm not saying Andreas is a bad guy, I'm just saying something feels weird about this whole thing. Something feels off."

Eric considered for a long moment. "Everything seems off right now." The confession hurt. "But out of all the people in this world, you're probably the last one to make something up just for the pleasure of my company."

Dan scoffed. "Yeah, no. The only concern I have is for Ada."

"I feel the same way." Eric met Dan's eyes. "I've been successful so far in managing my own privacy and security, but I had very little to offer my father's family in terms of the succession. Ada changes everything."

"I'll call my boss and let him know I need to stick around for a little while."

Eric watched him go. He'd be looking into Dan, too, and into his security firm. If everything checked out, he might have a solution that worked for everyone.

Chapter four

Dan woke up in a strange bed. It wasn't exactly out of the ordinary for him. His years in the Army made long-term relationships a challenge at best, and he'd traveled enough with Five Star that he hadn't exactly gotten around to fixing those tendencies in himself. This bed was a little more upscale than the type that usually housed his one-night stands, but whatever. He certainly wasn't about to complain about sheets with a high thread count or memory foam.

Of course, when Dan woke up in a strange bed, he didn't usually wake up alone.

That was when everything from the past two days came crashing back down on him. The call he'd gotten in Denver. The flight back to Boston. Fighting with the lawyers. That goddamned, stuck-up, beautiful-as-sin brother of Selene's . . .

Right. Beautiful as sin and kind enough to let Dan occupy a room in his house. The kind of guy who could openly admit to his shortcomings without flinching, and then take steps to fill in whatever gaps remained. The kind of guy who could recognize a threat and take whatever action he had to in order to protect a niece he hadn't even known existed when he woke up in the morning. The kind of guy who gave Dan an open ear and open mind, even though Dan had been a complete dick to him all day long.

Oh yeah. *Eric.* It didn't matter how kind he could be right now. He still came from that nest of vipers in Corvia. He'd turn around and bite eventually.

He groaned and pulled the covers back up. He wasn't ready for this, not today.

Then he rolled out of the luxurious bed all of Eric's royal money had provided, and hit the shower. He didn't have the luxury of hiding, of processing his grief and mourning the two lives that had been lost too soon. Ben and Selene were gone; their ordeal was over. Ada was what was important now.

Once Dan was clean and dressed, he found his way downstairs. Ada was awake, because all kids were early risers. Right now, she was coloring quietly at the table while Hadiya fixed breakfast and Eric read quietly to Ada from a tablet. He seemed much more comfortable with her now than

44

he had yesterday. Dan had to admit the sight wasn't unattractive.

Hadiya glowered at Dan, but she turned and offered him a cup of coffee. "I'll get you something to eat."

Dan took the cup. "Whatever you're cooking smells great. Sorry I wasn't up early enough to help."

Eric gave him a wry grin. "You'd just had a shock to your system, and from what your boss told me, you probably hadn't slept the night before. You needed the rest. Besides, it's not your job."

Hadiya passed him a jug of milk from the refrigerator. She didn't exactly give off the most welcoming vibe, but at least she didn't yell at him.

He turned to Eric instead of trying to butter up the housekeeper. "You spoke to Levi?"

"I did. He called me, actually. He mentioned you'd spoken about the situation here. We discussed a few options. I think you'll be hearing from him today." He tightened his jaw. "Whether that's before or after my brother's visit, I couldn't begin to guess."

Ada dropped her crayon. "I don't like him!" She glared at Eric. "I don't want him here."

Eric gave her a little grin. "I think it's safe to say I'd rather not have certain visitors at a time like this. Sometimes though, we need to do things that make us a little bit uncomfortable to get something we need."

Dan frowned. "Is that the best message?" He hoped his tone conveyed that the question was rhetorical and the answer was no.

Eric's grin turned sly. "Well, think of it this way. I don't want to make anyone unsafe. I'm not talking about anything like that. But Miss Ava, even though we don't want to have a visitor right now, we know it's unusual for him to want to come visit, right?"

Ada nodded, but the suspicion never left her face.

"Well, I want to know what's on his mind. It's probably going to be something that I need to know about, only to keep myself and you safe. So if I meet with him, even though I don't want to, I can find out what he wants and then do something to stop it."

Ada relaxed. "Mom says you're some kind of genius. Are you really?"

Eric's cheeks turned pink. "That's what they tell me. But the truth is, you're just as smart. And so is Hadiya, and so is your Uncle Dan. It's just a different way of using the brain." Eric ruffled her hair, which made Ada beam with delight.

Dan wasn't sure what the weird feeling in his chest was, and he knew he didn't much like it.

46

Somehow, the ugly stuck-up accent that made his skin crawl yesterday was giving him a different reaction today, and that was just weird.

"What's on today's agenda?" he asked to distract himself. "Other than a possible visit from Prince Andreas?"

Eric tilted his head. "Oh. I hadn't thought that far. I assume there will be coloring, perhaps some math?"

Hadiya scoffed and deposited a plate of food in front of Dan. "She's too young for math. She's old enough to play and to be read to."

"Surely —" Eric stopped himself. "Of course. You know how these things work. What do you think is best for her? I'm sure Ada here will probably get bored with her coloring book eventually."

"Do you have any dolls?" Ada pushed her coloring book away, as if on cue.

Dan frowned at her. "I brought your toys over yesterday. You have all of your dolls from your parents' house."

"I know." Ada sighed and wandered toward the door. "Hey, who's that guy?"

Dan jumped to his feet, putting himself between Hadiya and the window without thinking about it. "Do you have any workers coming over today?"

47

"No." Eric's jawline hardened. "Ada, with me, please."

Dan didn't have time to mess around with whatever the hell Eric thought he was going to do. Maybe *that guy* was just a nosy neighbor or something, but all of his senses were screaming that this was something real. He hadn't survived as long as he had by ignoring the hints his body gave him.

He opened the window Ada had looked through and jumped through it. The man had been hiding in a thorny hedge just outside the window, one Dan now jumped into. Dan had plunged into worse situations. It didn't take him long to realize his quarry probably hadn't. While the intruder had a head start, he seemed to be picking his way through the brambles away from the house while Dan just ran right at him.

Dan didn't tackle him until he made it to the lawn though. He wanted answers, not to torture the guy.

His prize turned out to be a middle-aged white man with a black hairy mole the size of a quarter on his right cheek.

"What the fuck, buddy?" The stranger squirmed ineffectively under Dan as Dan bound his arms behind him. Dan hadn't even realized he'd brought cuffs with him, but apparently, he'd subconsciously prepared for action today. "I ain't

48

broken no laws, pal. And mind the camera, it's expensive."

Dan glanced at the camera lying beside his prisoner, attached by a cord. "I'll bet." He hauled the stranger to his feet, camera and all. "And peeping in people's windows to take pictures of kids is, in fact, a crime."

"Hey, screw you, buddy. That kid's a princess. It's different rules for royalty."

Dan's blood ran cold. He wouldn't let this maggot see his bewilderment, but it was way too soon to hear any of that. "Actually, it isn't *different for royalty*, and my client will absolutely be pressing charges."

"Your client, huh?" The photographer struggled as Dan dragged him toward the house. "I'm pressing charges for kidnapping. And would that *client* be a royal himself?"

"That client is the dude paying my salary. And if I were you, I'd shut my cakehole."

The police showed up two minutes after Dan got the guy inside. At first, the paparazzo, whose ID claimed his name to be Archibald O'Reilly, tried to use the excuse of the free press. When one of the cops, a young Black woman who was almost too short for the job, pointed out that the free press did not extend to being a Peeping Tom and getting creeper shots of little girls in their homes, he demanded a lawyer.

"Where is the little darling anyway?" he asked, looking around. "If I'm going to have to put up with the police and all, I should at least get to meet her."

"Nope. Nothing doing." Dan had no idea where any of the home's actual residents had gone, but he'd happily block this jerk from moving even half an inch farther. "You have no rights with regard to that kid."

"How about the pretty boy I saw her with, huh? Think he'd answer a few questions for me?" O'Reilly wagged his eyebrows.

"That right to remain silent should be looming large in your mind right now." The larger male cop hauled O'Reilly toward the door. "Oh, and your ladder and camera are both evidence now. Good times."

Dan called the incident in as the officers drove away with the prisoner. He didn't know what kind of arrangement Eric and Levi had made, but he wanted some kind of record of the incident just in case.

Levi sighed when Dan finished his tale. "I wish I could say I was surprised. Eric's managed to stay off the radar for years, and so did Selene. She was able to keep that kid out of the press completely, which feels like nothing short of a miracle. But after speaking with Eric, I almost expected something like this to happen. I'll look into the guy. Don't be too shocked if it comes back to something shady."

"Don't they always." Dan glared at the door. "The last thing I want is for my niece to have to grow up in some kind of dark fortress. Why would the press suddenly have an interest in her?"

Levi hesitated, and Dan could hear him typing away. "Well, for one thing, Selene kept them away. For another, it seems like the royals back in the old country are giving the press plenty to talk about. Apparently, they're the scandal of Europe. King Sebastian got caught having an affair with a woman younger than Eric there, and got her pregnant. Wifey number four is furious, she's also pregnant, and Eric's older brother Hans got caught smuggling heroin into Russia. That would be Selene's younger brother."

"Charming." These Adlers should have all been drowned at birth. Why hadn't that happened again?

It occurred to Dan that Eric might be an exception to that rule, but he couldn't be sure. Not yet.

"Most of this stuff is in German or French, but I can see why some of the English-language press is picking up on it. People love a good scandal, especially when it comes to royalty. And I can see why certain other royals would be over the moon at having a sweet, young, scandal-free royal to trot out and make people happy over."

"Justifying their paycheck for yet another generation." Dan rubbed at his face. "Christ, I hate this crap."

"Well, this crap is paying for you to stick around in Boston. I can send someone else, but I figured you'd want the assignment. She's your niece." Levi chuckled. "I mean you'd be on family leave otherwise, which isn't an issue, but we both know you wouldn't trust anyone else with your family."

Dan snorted. "Yeah, I know." He sighed. "And Eric's not bad, for a royal. He's probably not all that enthusiastic about any of this himself. I'm just being an ass."

"Uncle Dan said a bad word!" Ada hadn't developed any kind of volume control yet, so Levi probably could have heard her in Colorado even without the phone. "Uncle Dan said a bad word for butt!"

Levi burst out laughing in Dan's ear even as Dan turned to see Eric standing there, a weird little smirk on his face as he leaned in the doorway.

"Crap, I've got to go. I'll talk to you later." He hung up. "How much of that did you hear?"

Eric winked and headed into one of the excessive parlors, the one that seemed the least formal. "Enough to know I'm not bad for a royal." Then he laughed quietly. "Honestly, I think that's the nicest thing anyone's ever said about me."

Ada stomped her foot. "I don't want to be a princess. I want to be a hockey player!"

Eric patted the sofa and sat on it, Ada climbing onto it beside him. "Ada, my love, I'm afraid being a princess is something you're born with. It's like having pale skin or red hair. It's just something that's in your background because of who your mother and your grandparents were. It doesn't mean you can't be a hockey player. It just means there are going to be occasional jerks around who want to take pictures of you, and that's all." He turned to Dan and met his eyes.

"Where did you guys get to?" Dan had to say something, or else he was at real risk of getting lost in those dark orbs. "When I got back inside, it was like none of you had ever been here."

"Uncle Eric has a secret room!" Ada jumped up and down in delight. "He says it's very old, and they used to hide people in it when they were trying to escape from slavery. And there was writing on the wall, and there was an old bottle he didn't even know was in there, but he wouldn't let me drink from it—"

Eric blushed. "Apparently, the house has a history. I found the secret room when I was house hunting, and I'll admit it played a role in my choice of homes. I didn't realize it had been a home to bootleggers too."

Dan exhaled and tried to push his bad feelings out with his breath. "I'd love to see it."

Chapter five

Nausea burned its way up Eric's throat as he stared down at his phone. He'd gotten a one-day reprieve from his older brother's visit. He supposed he should be grateful for the extra twenty-four hours, but instead, he simply wanted to throw up. Growing up, Andreas had been his bogeyman, his devil, his monster under the bed. Somehow, Eric didn't think their relationship would change just because of shared grief.

Although, given that Eric hadn't known his sister was in the area and Andreas had the emotional capacity of the average wounded and rabid wolverine, perhaps *grief* was an overstatement.

"They're only a few minutes out." He looked up at the rest of the crowd.

Dan Marshall was there, officially representing Five Star Security. Fred Hargrove was there too, continuing to represent Selene's interests as well as those of Ada. Eric had called in his own attorneys, Kristin Ainsley and Florian Rodriguez. The three lawyers stood in a little clump near the bar, mixing their own drinks and chatting.

Dr. Omar, from the school, was there too. Dan had suggested it, since he'd done so well with Ada. Eric had agreed to it, although he'd been surprised when Omar accepted. He stood near Hadiya, who had a monitor clipped to her belt. She could hear anything happening upstairs.

"Does your brother typically text you when he's close?" Omar tilted his head, curious.

"My guess is that he wants to minimize any fuss that would draw attention." Dan stepped in smoothly, as though he'd ever met Andreas before. If he had, he'd have known Andreas lived for the attention he got as a royal. He thrived on the "fuss."

Then again, Andreas was showing up under cover of darkness, and news of his arrival hadn't been spread through the media. Maybe there was something to what Dan was saying after all.

The sound of not one but three vehicles in the driveway interrupted Eric's tense musings, and he got up. "Sounds as if the guest of the hour is here." He aimed himself for the door, but Dan stopped him.

56

"Pretty sure that's the kind of thing you're paying me for," he said with a big sigh, and opened the front door for him.

Eric's cheeks burned, but he didn't correct Dan. He didn't want to undermine him in front of all of these people, especially since he knew perfectly well how it felt. He cast his gaze toward the bar and wished he had a drink in his hand, more for something to do with it than anything else.

With Dr. Omar in the house, he couldn't let himself indulge. He wasn't a particularly observant Muslim, and barely considered himself to be part of the faith at all, but he wasn't going to outright insult his guest under the circumstances. If he were more of a drinker, maybe he'd reconsider. As it was, he wanted to be more considerate.

And, of course, he wanted to keep every last one of his wits about him with Andreas on the scene.

The first person to enter was clearly someone from the American diplomatic services. Eric recognized the suit, the haircut, and the earpiece. Two older men, also in suits, followed, and then Andreas.

Andreas was Andreas. He never changed, or at least if he did change, it was never more than superficial. His wide strong jaw was softened somewhat by the lightest of goatees, even lighter than his artfully messy blond hair. He must be dying it now, at least some of the time. Andreas was probably nearing forty.

His suit could have paid for the clothes worn by everyone else in the room five times over, and the way he looked Eric's cohort over told him he knew it. His icy blue eyes took in the assembled guests, and he curled his lip when he recognized Dan.

"Daniel Marshall. Back from fighting other people's wars for them?"

Dan didn't react. He simply stood by the door and waited for the other man from Diplomatic Security to follow Andreas inside. Then he closed and secured the door behind him.

If Andreas was expecting people to bow or otherwise acknowledge his position, he would be sorely disappointed. No one did anything of the sort. Eric gestured to the bar. "Drinks are over there, brother. I'm sure you can mix your own, far better than I ever could."

Andreas strode toward the bar. "You really should invest in a staff, and I don't mean that wretched girl from the Emirates. She's not good for anything—maybe a little bit of family cookery, but you're a prince. You need someone who's capable of entertaining on a larger scale. You need people who can serve your guests and clean up after them."

Eric rolled his eyes and shook his head. He didn't ask how his brother knew about Hadiya. He didn't want to know. "I don't entertain much. It's not a lifestyle I've ever aspired to, Andreas. Hadiya is enough for me. I'll need to get a nanny for Ada, but it's only been two days. There's time enough to find someone safe who will be able to meet all of her needs."

Andreas completely ignored the lawyers at the bar while mixing his gimlet. "Nonsense. She'll be returning with me. I'm sure you see reason by now, after a day to process the shock. Selene hated you. She wouldn't want her child to have anything to do with you. If she had, she'd have introduced you before she perished so terribly." He glanced at Dan and waved a hand. "I mean, Mr. Marshall here would be a more suitable guardian, not that I'd tolerate that any more than I'm tolerating this. At least he was at the wedding."

Dan stared Andreas down with as stony a face as any statue, any monument.

Fred cleared his throat. "Perhaps your Highness is correct about my client's relationship with her brother, but the fact remains that the will is true. Both she and her husband signed it in my office, in my presence, in front of witnesses and a video camera."

Rodriguez, who handled most of Eric's financial issues, turned to Fred. "You recorded the will on video?"

Fred nodded slowly, like some old sage in a fantasy movie instead of the middle-aged law partner he was. "Mrs. Marshall felt it would be appropriate, all things considered. She wanted to make sure her wishes could not be contravened."

Andreas' face went red, but for just a moment.

Then one of the men in suits with him, almost certainly an attorney, stepped in. "Of course, I can understand taking such a step. However, under Corvian law, the wishes of the Crown quite naturally overrule the wishes of a subject. And Princess Selene, while a member of the royal family, remains a subject."

Omar set his jaw. Eric didn't think he'd ever seen a cleric so ready to throw a punch before.

He intervened before he had to explain to the university why their cleric had been arrested. "Naturally. And were we in Corvia, I would have no problem yielding to the law there. That said, Ada is an American citizen, not Corvian. She was born here, not in Corvia, and her parents were killed on American soil, not Corvian soil. I'm not an attorney—"

"You have a law degree from Yale," Hadiya interrupted him. "You *teach* law."

"I have some passing familiarity with the law," Eric corrected, without missing a beat, "but I am not an expert in estate planning or family law. I'll defer to Ms. Ainsley and Mr. Rodriguez, who are. I don't think it's going too far out on a limb to assume that American laws apply here in Massachusetts."

Ainsley grinned the vicious smile he'd hired her for and stepped up, martini in hand. "Of course, Dr. Alawi. The precedent was established very clearly in *Kent v. Fujimori*—"

Andreas' other lawyer, who turned out to be American by the sound of him, shook his head. "That's a completely different situation. That's a biological parent seeking to recover children taken illegally and against their will—"

Eric tuned them out. The American lawyer was in the wrong for interrupting Ainsley, but she'd make him regret it before the night was through. If he understood the gleam in her eyes, he might regret it before Andreas finished his drink.

Andreas seemed to be tuning the lawyers out as well. "You understand, of course, that nothing will be decided tonight. This girl is my own

61

flesh and blood. I have a right to see her and to know her. And Father—he was heartbroken after Selene married that carpenter's son."

Dan stiffened, just a little bit. If Eric hadn't been standing so close to him, he'd never have noticed.

"I wouldn't know. I was pretty well out of the loop by that point, I'm afraid—which can't be helped now, I suppose. How is he?"

"Well, he's beside himself with grief, of course. Selene always was his favorite, and she certainly can't ask his forgiveness now." Andreas closed his eyes and sipped from his drink. "It's so sad to see a family torn apart like this. You're over here, you live in hiding, you won't even use his last name."

"I believe that was his request." Eric shrugged. "It does work out well for me, as I've managed to avoid some of the less savory aspects of media exposure by keeping my mother's name." He forced a bland smile onto his face. His mother had been just as happy to be rid of him as his father, but he'd never give Andreas that kind of ammunition. "And he has plenty of other children."

"But only one grandchild to give him comfort. The child would bring him so much delight, especially to have her reared properly as is

62

her birthright. Not here, in some backwater." Andreas shook his head. "I do believe I was making some headway with Selene before her demise. She was a thousand times more stubborn than you. I know you'll see things my way soon enough." He tossed his head back and finished his drink in one fell swoop. "We'll speak again, little brother."

Andreas headed for the door without another word, leaving it to his retinue to catch up.

In only a few seconds, only Eric's team was left. Andreas' lawyers left behind half-finished drinks, suddenly quiet spaces, and a lot of unanswered questions.

Rodriguez broke the silence first. "Well, that was exciting. Are your meetings together always this warm and fuzzy?"

"He broke my nose once." Eric shrugged. "There's probably video somewhere." For a moment, shame and anger flooded through him.

He locked them back down. This wasn't the time or place for such things. For one thing, this was supposed to be time for Ada, not for Eric's family issues. He'd been apart from family his entire life. He didn't need to be the focus of their attention now, as an adult, with a small child who needed so much from everyone.

For another, no one had cared about his family issues back when they'd been fresh and raw

63

and bleeding. Expecting anyone to care about them now was like expecting someone to suddenly become passionate about a centuries-old internecine conflict between two long-extinct populations—an interesting thought exercise, but not something to be hoped for.

He cleared away the drinks and the napkins as his attorneys talked strategy, Dr. Omar and Hadiya discussed strategies for Ada, and Dan did whatever Dan did.

Oh—Dan was following him into the kitchen. "I've got to say, I've never seen royalty clean up after their own houseguests. Except Selene, I guess, and it even took her a while to figure out how to do it."

Eric bit down on the inside of his cheek. Dan was probably trying to give him a compliment. "I was brought up very differently from my siblings—on both sides, I should say. Children in boarding schools learn independence at a fairly young age, I'm afraid." He forced himself to grin. "I have to apologize for Andreas' comments. I didn't know there was any bad blood about the wedding, but I suppose I shouldn't be surprised."

"It's nothing he didn't say at the time. A few of them had comments to make. Let's just say I was already not the biggest fan of royalty before the whole thing." He scratched at his head. "I'd been in

64

a couple of situations, here and there. Rangers don't show up to see anyone on their best days, you know?"

Eric did not know, but he'd take Dan's word for it. "I suppose you don't. And I know the Corvian royal family wouldn't have shown you their best side anyway. When I was younger, I resented being kept away. Now that I'm older, I'm grateful." He laughed ruefully. "I feel bad because it sounds like Selene turned into a nice person after all that, and I missed out. I feel bad for Ada most of all. I'll be the first to admit I'm not exactly a 'kid' person, and the trauma to Ada is compounded by being sent off to live with some freak with a secret room in his walls. But I don't miss dealing with the Corvian royals at all."

"I can't imagine how anyone would." Dan shuddered. "But then again, Selene did turn out okay. And apparently, she knew you did too." He put a hand on Eric's shoulder and then brushed his lips across Eric's.

Chapter Six

Dan kicked himself all night long, in the privacy of his too-luxurious bedroom. Why had he kissed Eric? It must have been that moment when his eyes had flashed, mentioning the broken nose. For just one blink-and-you'll-miss-it second, Eric's cool, detached facade had broken. Dan had been allowed to see inside and witness the very lonely man underneath.

It couldn't have anything to do with his full lips, the light stubble on his cheeks, or the loose black curls just begging someone to run their fingers through them.

Eric played a prominent role in Dan's dreams that night, which was just embarrassing. Thankfully, he was able to get himself cleaned up and dressed before Ada burst into the bedroom with one of those hotel breakfast bar single-serving boxes of cereal. "I brought you breakfast, Uncle Dan!"

He caught her up in a massive hug and spun her around in a circle, the way she'd always liked. She rewarded his efforts with shrieks and giggles.

"How about if we go downstairs and eat this in the kitchen? I'm sure your Uncle Eric wouldn't like it if we got crumbs all over the place and attracted mice."

Ada wrinkled her little brow and put her hand in his. "But Uncle Eric said I could bring it to you. He made me wait until the water wasn't running anymore though. Said it wasn't polite."

Dan blushed. "Well, grown-ups have a thing about privacy. When we're washing up, we don't want people to see us naked—especially not kids. It's kind of gross."

"I'm still too little to wash myself. But someday I can have piracy too." Ada beamed, proud of herself.

Dan had to restrain himself from laughing at the mistake in her words.

Eric didn't mention the kiss when he got downstairs, but Dan didn't think he would. Not in front of Ada or Hadiya.

Eric had dispensed with the suit and tie for the morning. He wore a Harvard T-shirt and a pair of sweatpants, both of which had generous servings of suds on them as well. Dan had to look away. Not only did Eric have a pretty hot body

68

underneath all the formal clothing, but he didn't seem to be flinching away from the mess breakfast had made of the kitchen.

He must have picked up on Dan's glance, somehow, because he grinned wryly and got back to scrubbing pots. "Apologies for the informal attire. I thought it best to scrub in something that didn't require dry cleaning."

"They do say you're a genius." Dan sat down at the end of the table and fought to will his growing erection away.

Just as he finally achieved success, Ada climbed into his lap. Dan had always had great timing.

"One does one's best. If one can't learn from one's first destroyed sport coat, when can one learn?"

Dan chuckled, but he tilted his head to the side as Hadiya brought over a plate of French toast. "Don't take this the wrong way, but I didn't expect you to be the pot-scrubbing type."

Hadiya blushed and turned her head away, but Eric just shook his head. "Hadiya got up early to cook something she isn't used to because she wanted to make Ada smile. And it was a very good breakfast, but it did get somewhat messy. Since Hadiya went to all the trouble of cooking, I certainly don't mind being the one to scrub up—

especially as I'm on family leave." He gave a little laugh. "I think Miss Ada might be good for me. I'd normally have to go and have a lie-down if the kitchen were this untidy, but here I am washing up with joy in my heart."

"What about me?" Ada pouted, hands on her hips.

"Oh, my Ada." Eric's smile was fond as he shifted a little to face her. "For one thing, you haven't made any huge messes, don't worry about that. I'm sure you will because you're four and that's evidently normal. I looked it up.

"I was quite worried, you see. Because of the way I grew up, I tend to be upset when I see messes. And I was afraid I'd get upset because of things that are normal, things you can't control and shouldn't have to. But here I am, just enjoying your company and wanting to find ways to make you happy. You're a strong little girl, Ada. I'm so proud to be your uncle. I can't wait to get to know you better."

Ada ducked her head, so her long red hair hid her face. Dan knew his niece though. He knew she was blushing.

"You mean it? Even though I yelled at you when we first met?"

"No one can be mad at you for that, sweetheart." Eric hadn't stopped scrubbing. Now he cleansed the last of the filth off the pan and let it

70

sink back into the suds. "It was a scary situation, and you'd just been through something terrible. I was a stranger. I'd have yelled at me too."

A little voice deep inside Dan poked him. *That's why you kissed him.*

He cleared his throat. Thinking about kissing, in any way at all, wasn't going to help keep Ada safe. "So, do you think you could make the time to sit down with me and talk some things through with Levi? I want to talk about last night's meeting, maybe make some plans. If that's okay."

Eric looked over at Hadiya. "Is there a time that works for you? I don't want to presume you're open to this. I know you didn't sign on for childcare."

Hadiya laughed. "I don't mind watching her for an hour or two here and there, or pitching in and helping out when things need to get done. I'm not qualified to watch her all day while you're at work, but I'm happy to help out when I can."

"Thank you, Hadiya. Maybe after I'm done with the dishes?"

Dan could get behind that. He reached out to Levi to make sure he was available, and then when everyone had been fed and caffeinated, he and Eric retreated to Eric's home office.

Eric's office looked more like a microlibrary. Every wall was covered in floor-to-ceiling bookshelves. He had a large solid-wood desk, with a laptop on it and a single coaster. Nothing was out of place.

He hadn't been kidding when he said a kid should be making him tear his hair out.

Eric excused himself to get a chair for Dan, giving him a chance to look around. The books on the shelves came in a variety of languages, some of which Dan recognized. One section was dedicated to law books. Some were about engineering, others about chemistry. Some focused on history, others on government or religion. Some were in English, others in Arabic, some in German or French. Some were in Latin. Others—well, Dan wasn't even going to try.

Dan huffed out a laugh. Selene had mentioned her brother was "some kind of genius," but he'd dismissed it. Apparently, Selene hadn't been kidding.

Eric returned with a chair and his usual formal attire. "It felt disrespectful," he said with a shrug.

Dan hadn't said anything, but he figured his disappointment must have shown in his eyes.

"Don't some of your students wear their actual pajamas to class?"

"Well, yes, but that's them. We had to wear a full suit and tie to so much as scratch our noses.

It's a difficult habit to break. Anything less feels like showing up naked. I suppose there's a time and a place for anything, but security discussions aren't it."

Dan took the seat Eric offered, hoping it would hide his reaction. *He did that on purpose.* "I don't know. Maybe it's exactly the right place to show up naked."

"Perhaps next time." Humor danced behind Eric's eyes as he opened up the video chat with Levi.

Levi looked tired, but then again Levi probably had a lot on his plate. "Good morning, gentlemen. How are things going in scenic Beantown?"

"Eric here's got Ada eating out of his hands already." Dan smirked. "Of course, she was supposed to be eating with a fork, but we'll get there eventually."

Eric snickered. "In all seriousness, Mr. Marshall has been of invaluable assistance, both with Ada and with security. I'm sure you've already heard about the paparazzo, and then, of course, last night we had a visit from my charming brother."

"That would be Prince Andreas." Levi nodded. "Yes, Dan updated me. Your paparazzo made bail, but a judge issued a formal gag order on sharing the location of your home on the basis of your niece's privacy. How are you going to handle getting her into school or day care?"

"I'm not going to have to go back to work until September, thankfully, but I'd like to get a childcare professional integrated into the household before then. It will likely take some time to find someone suitable. May I call on your organization to help with background checks? I'm likely to reach out to my stepbrother, on my mother's side, first. He's helped me before, finding people who needed to leave their country who wouldn't object to my particular quirks. In an ideal situation, I'd want to find someone in a similar situation."

Dan didn't need any more information to know he was talking about Hadiya.

"Sure. Just let me know. In the meantime, I wanted to give you an update about the accident that started everything." Levi glanced away. "This isn't easy."

Dan glanced at Eric, who looked as perplexed as Dan felt. "What's going on, Levi?"

"Well, you see . . ." Levi ran his hand over his face, and the image glitched for a second. "I've heard from the state police investigators. Apparently, the car that hit the Marshalls was completely clean."

74

Dan's blood ran cold.

Eric frowned and leaned forward. "You're speaking forensically, not in terms of cleanliness at all."

"Correct. There were no hairs, no fingerprints, no fibers that didn't come from inside the car itself. In fact, they couldn't find any hints that any human had been inside the car at all."

"I didn't believe self-driving cars were able to be harnessed in that way." Eric spoke after only a second. The only way Dan knew he was affected by the information at all was in the sudden pallor of his skin.

"Typically, they aren't. There are always bad actors who would like them to be, of course, and organizations who are willing to play with them until they are." Levi sighed heavily, and Dan's phone buzzed with an incoming message. "Dan, I've sent you some video. It's from traffic light cameras. The vehicle that hit them accelerated through three red lights before smashing into the driver's side at one hundred miles per hour."

"Christ." Dan couldn't lose it. He couldn't run into the lavish guest bathroom and return his single-serving Honey Smacks. He'd seen the horrors of war firsthand, witnessed things so terrible, he hesitated sometimes to even be around his niece. He hadn't even glimpsed Ben's remains. He could get through this discussion.

"The child survived because Selene invested in the very best child safety equipment she could, to include the vehicle itself. Eric, I've sent you the make and model. I can't recommend it highly enough, or the safety seats. The important thing to remember right now, though, is that this is looking like a homicide."

Eric exhaled slowly. "I see. Do they have suspects?"

"They're not ruling anyone out. Except you, because you didn't know they even lived in the area. Selene's position means she was the likely target, and not Ben, but that's probably cold comfort to you, Dan."

"Yeah. But, ah." Dan covered his mouth. "Sorry. I just need a few seconds."

"Whatever you need." Levi paused. "They're not going to come to you—either of you— with this until they have more information. They may just kick it up to the feds because of the delicate international situation."

"They don't want a princess' death being investigated by anything but what's perceived as top-level investigators." Eric rolled his eyes so hard Dan wondered if they were going to pop out. "Apologies. I know there are some concerns at work when dealing with crimes involving foreign dignitaries, even those who've abandoned the concept." He took a deep breath. "I've been somewhat out of the loop when it comes to Corvian politics, so I'm unable to assist. Andreas was in Washington until yesterday or possibly the day before, I believe."

"That's not exactly true." Levi sipped from a cup of coffee. "Prince Andreas has been in Boston for two weeks. His security detail is usually pretty good about keeping his location under wraps, but his blog logs his location when he posts. It doesn't *reveal* his location, but we've got a guy here who can find it, and believe me when I tell you, he's been in Boston at the Boston Harbor Hotel."

Dan stared at his boss. "What are you trying to say?"

"Just that Andreas—sorry, Prince Andreas—adds a level of complexity to the investigation. Investigators have to be very careful when asking him questions. They can't arrest him, or even threaten to arrest him. He's the crown prince of Corvia, not some dipshit rich kid in over his head." Levi sighed.

"He can be both." Eric drummed his fingers on the desk. "I can't bring myself to believe Andreas would stoop to something so low, but it's worth looking into his activity. He's very insistent on bringing Ada back to Corvia, which is something her mother clearly didn't want. I wouldn't . . ." He trailed off, eyes far away. "It's possible he said the wrong thing in front of the wrong person, I suppose.

"And you don't have to refer to him as Prince Andreas, not in front of me. I moved to America specifically because we don't *have* royalty here. Yes, it's his preference, and if that's your choice, then by all means, continue. Please don't do it because you think I'm getting hung up on it."

Levi grinned. "Fair point. I wanted to make sure you guys were updated on the situation. Anyway, I've got to run. I've got another client whose case is about to close spectacularly, but it's going to take a certain amount of finesse."

"Is this the one Jamal's on?" Dan perked up. Jamal had gotten assigned to a case out in California and last Dan had heard, the poor guy was miserable out there.

"The very same. I'll catch up with you two later."

Levi hung up, and Dan turned to Eric. "How are you holding up?"

Eric wrinkled his nose. "I should be asking you that question. You signed on to help manage things like paparazzi, not to risk your life." He hesitated, and then he put his hand on Dan's shoulder. "I'm so sorry. Whatever the real story is, proximity to my family caused harm to yours. None of you chose to expose yourself to this."

Dan lowered his gaze. He couldn't deny what Eric was saying. "No one does, I guess."

Chapter Seven

Eric stayed in his office for a while after Dan staggered out. He considered following him. That kiss must have meant something, after all. Even if it hadn't, Dan was a guest in his home and was clearly not reacting well to the news of their siblings' murder. Who would?

You would because they're strangers and could never be anything else.

He pushed the negative thought away. He was shocked, yes. And he wanted to comfort Dan, but Dan didn't want comfort from him. And what kind of comfort could Eric give, really? Dan's beloved brother had just been murdered because he'd been married to Eric's sister, and for no other reason. Even if Eric had ever been able to offer much comfort to anyone, Dan would be the absolute last person to find him helpful right now.

And so he sent an email to his stepbrother. Ali had been perhaps ten when his father had married Eric's mother. Eric had been five. They hadn't been particularly close, nor had anyone encouraged them to become close, but Eric supposed he was the closest of all Eric's siblings. He was kind, and he didn't judge, and he reached out at Ramadan. It was enough for Eric.

Ali had married into the royal family, one of the king's nieces. It got him a position as Deputy Finance Minister, which put him into a position to help cautiously guide the kingdom into a better position for the future. The king was on board. So was the crown prince. They'd even gone so far as to adopt some of Eric's energy and desalinization solutions.

All of them, unfortunately, had to walk a delicate path. Fundamentalists had gained a secure foothold in the kingdom, and no one wanted to piss them off or see what happened if their power grew. Eric couldn't return because his outing had caused enough of a stir in Corvia that the fundamentalists knew about it. Ali didn't care, the prince didn't care, the king didn't care, but Eric still had to stay away.

Ali, being a smart man, had recognized the opportunity in having a stepbrother living in exile with access to diplomatic channels for three countries. He called Eric from time to time with cases of people who needed to leave the country,

82

usually in a hurry. Eric rarely had trouble finding places for them. Hadiya had been one of them. Another of them was enrolled in the Chemistry department at the university. Eric saw him regularly.

Ali called him right away. "Eric, brother, how are you?" Ali always sounded happy to hear from him, even though they hadn't seen each other face-to-face in a decade at least. "I hope you've found someone to settle down with at last. Even though you can't bring him here, perhaps I can come there to meet him in person."

Eric blushed. Ali always said things like that. "I'm afraid it's not like that. The news still hasn't been released, but my father's eldest daughter was killed a few days ago in a car accident."

Ali gasped. "That's terrible! I remember when we got the news about her wedding. She had a child, didn't she?"

And of course, even his stepbrother knew more about Eric's bio family than he did. Even his stepbrother was welcome to know more. "She did. A daughter, four years old and possibly the strongest child in history." He grimaced ruefully. "And Selene left her in my care."

Ali fell silent for a good ten seconds. Then he laughed. "I'm sorry. I'm so sorry—it's not a laughing matter. But you have to admit, the thought is . . ."

"Absurd, yes." Eric had to grin. "The chaplain at the university has stepped in to help, as have Hadiya and Ada's paternal uncle. It seems even a soldier is more competent to care for a child than I am. But it's obvious I won't be able to care for her alone. Especially . . ."

"Yes?"

"There's reason to believe her parents' death may not have been an accident. I don't want to look locally for a nanny under the circumstances."

"I see." Eric heard Ali typing. "I have a few people I can speak with. I'll make some inquiries and see what I can do." He paused. "I'm very sorry for your loss. I know you weren't particularly close, but it still must be difficult for you."

Eric bowed his head. "Thank you. Ada is the one I feel sorriest for. She's resilient, but I know how keenly she feels the loss."

"It isn't as though you don't have experience there yourself. Please let her know she has a much larger extended family who loves and cares for her too, now. If there is anything I can do to help you or her, don't hesitate to say the word."

"I won't." Eric smiled, even though he knew Ali couldn't see him. "Thank you for your help."

He intended to go back downstairs when the call ended, but his phone rang again. This number could bring no smile to his face. Eric had never dialed it before, but he recognized it easily.

"Your Majesty." He swallowed hard and greeted his father. "I hope you're well."

"Well?" Sebastian, king of Corvia, snarled his words into the phone. "How can I be well when the princess royal is dead, her daughter is in captivity, and all of my children disappoint and disobey me?"

Eric pinched the bridge of his nose. "Ada isn't in captivity, Your Majesty. She's in the parlor. I believe her uncle is reading her a story." He was making the activity up, but someone would have interrupted his call if there was a problem with Ada. All Eric wanted to do was to get his father off the phone as quickly as he could. Besides, Ada liked being read to, even if Eric half suspected she could read most of those books herself.

"Is that so? You think she's free to return to Corvia? Then send her back this instant!"

Eric counted to five. "The terms of Selene's will are clear. I am obligated to keep Ada with me, or the consequences will be dire. I don't know why it was so important to her for me to keep Ada. I truly don't, sire, but under United States law I cannot contravene the terms of her will."

85

"So bring her back yourself. Then you're not disobeying her stupid will, and you're not disobeying your father and your king."

Eric sat up straighter. "Your Majesty was quite clear the last time I was in Corvia."

"Yes—step up and play your part. Do this, and you'll be welcome in your own country again. You've been skating by in obscurity thinking it's perfectly acceptable to go prancing around with men, corrupting the youth, teaching them blasphemy, and what the hell ever, when your country needs you at your brother's side, supporting him and helping to lead Corvia. I didn't sire some college professor, I sired a prince. Now get your well-used ass back here and act like one."

Eric ground his teeth together. "I will not. Nor will I subject that delightful child to the same ridiculous behavior. She's an American citizen. She is not subject to Corvian law."

"But you are not an American." Sebastian hung up, his implicit threat hanging in the air.

Eric pushed his phone away. It was too early in the day to start drinking, and he wasn't much of a drinker to begin with. That bottle of gin in the downstairs library was looking awful tempting though.

He hauled himself to his feet. None of this was supposed to be about him, and he needed to

86

get himself back into form before he saw Dan or Ada. Hadiya had seen Eric rattled before, but Ada was scared and traumatized and needed support and care. Dan was no less traumatized, for all his military experience. And someone out there had murdered Selene and might be coming for Ada.

He grabbed his phone again and typed out a quick message to Levi, updating him on the call from his father. He copied Dan on the message, not expecting any reply from either of them. He just wanted to make sure everyone had all the information. Then he checked to make sure his clothing wasn't too much of a mess, rechecked his desk to make sure it was tidy, and headed back downstairs.

When he got downstairs, Ada colored quietly on the floor. Hadiya sat nearby, scrolling through her tablet with a watchful eye on the little girl. Dan sat on the antique sofa, eyes far away, and didn't even look up when Eric stepped into the doorway. No one there needed him.

What had Eric been thinking? He was a placeholder, nothing more. No one had been waiting for him to do anything. No one needed his presence or wanted his company. Selene had chosen him because he was close by if anything happened and because, yes, he was good at staying off the radar. She hadn't chosen him because he was particularly beloved or admired.

He padded back toward the kitchen. He'd meant what he said to his father. He wasn't going to ship Ada to Corvia. He'd send her to Ali before he let her anywhere near Andreas, or Sebastian for that matter. On this, he knew the law was on his side. Selene's wishes were obvious and well-documented. The child was American born, which carried weight in cases like this. He could hand her over to Dan and make everyone much happier. To be sure, Selene's little poison pill would kick in, but he would work with his sister's former attorney to negate that provision first. Eric would cheerfully give Dan the house and fund them for the rest of their lives to boot.

The idea gave him a little pain, and he found it wasn't only because he'd been kissed last night. No, he'd gotten used to having them around the place. He didn't know why. He'd never seen himself as much of a family man, but they'd gotten under his skin in a way few people had. Perhaps it was the love they had for each other.

Maybe Eric saw a little bit of himself in Ada, lost and confused and grieving. He'd miss her.

He'd miss both of them, even though he'd only known them for a few short days. He'd sacrifice the pleasure of their company to keep

88

them safe and happy. He hadn't missed the threat in his father's words. He'd been living here for years, and he hadn't had any trouble at all with it, but he knew it could all go away in an instant.

Why would his father be so desperate to bring Ada to Corvia?

For that matter, why would Sebastian want Eric back in Corvia? Eric had been officially unwelcome in the kingdom of his birth since he'd been unceremoniously outed. He'd been unofficially unwelcome since his parents' divorce, when he was all of two. He felt less of a connection to Corvia than he did to Peru, and Sebastian hadn't gone to any length to change that.

Until today, if his ranting, shouting diatribe could be considered to be an invitation. Sebastian could be erratic on the best of days. Eric didn't pretend to know what went on in his head. Unfortunately, he needed to get a handle on it if he wanted to keep his ward out of harm's way.

He made his way back to his office and sighed. If he wasn't going to be useful with Ada, he might as well get some work done. He was officially on family leave, something he never thought he'd use, but that only meant he didn't need to be on campus or in front of students. He could still correspond with his mentees and do research. He could still publish.

He put the chair he'd brought for Dan across the room, rather than beside him, and tried not to think about the warmth of Dan's body against his skin. How foolish had he been to think he could ever attract someone like Dan? Eric had accepted his lot in life a long time ago. He needed to accept who and what he was, and just get on with life.

It wasn't even a bad life. He had more money than he knew what to do with. He had a home. He had a career he truly enjoyed, and not many people could make the same claim. He was able to use his privilege to help people who didn't have the same opportunities. Sure, he was lonely, but no one could expect to have everything in life. He needed to appreciate what he had and stop focusing on what he didn't.

He reached for his laptop and drafted a message to his attorneys. He had arrangements to make.

Chapter Eight

Dan had been looking forward to talking with Eric a little more, but once Ada went to bed Eric disappeared back to his office with a polite little smile and a *goodnight* that left Dan confused as hell. It was probably for the best, getting close to guys from his background never worked well, but still — what the hell?

As luck would have it though, his phone rang not long after Eric left him in the library. When Dan saw his parents' names flash across the screen, he almost dropped the phone. How in the hell had he not called them yet? Sure, they'd never been on great terms, but of all the times to hold a grudge, this was the worst.

"Hey." He didn't direct his answer toward a particular parent. Either one of them would be equally pissed.

"Daniel." Great. Dad was the one calling. Mom was probably just too pissed, and rightly so. "You'll never believe who just called me."

Dan took a deep breath and reminded himself that his father was grieving too. "Who, Dad?"

"The king of Corvia. He couldn't be bothered to call the day our children died, of course, but he was moved to call and *demand* that I exert my influence to get our grandchild sent to Corvia. Which is the first I heard that there was any kind of custody dispute going on at all. How in the hell did you screw this up?"

Dan stared at the wall, at books in languages he couldn't read and a fully-stocked bar. What the hell—Eric kept telling him to make himself at home. He headed over to the bar and made himself a gin and tonic as he replied to his father. "You know, I'm willing to take my share of the blame for how we got along—or didn't—when I was a kid. But this? This ain't my fault. This is on Selene and Ben. And after seeing what's going on, I don't necessarily disagree with them."

Dad scoffed. "Of course you don't. You're still the same snot-nosed little shit I sent off to the Army."

Dan took a swig from his glass and let the booze cut through the lump in his throat. "Maybe.

But at least my time in the Rangers taught me a hell of a lot about security. Selene and Ben didn't want their kid growing up in that nest of vipers, and they were right. So they left custody of that angel to someone who hates that king even more than Selene did. I don't know why, and I don't have to. He's got the means and the motive to keep Ada away from Corvia forever, if he has to."

"Sure, but he's going to keep her away from us too. That includes you. Don't think for a minute it doesn't." Dad slurped from a drink of his own. The way he slurred his words told Dan it probably wasn't his first drink.

Dan wasn't going to judge. Ted had just lost his beloved firstborn son and was left with only Dan now.

"Actually, Eric's only interest has been what's best for Ada. He hasn't wanted to separate me from her at all. He's letting me stay in his house while we work this whole mess out, and hired me for security purposes."

"Sure, for now. These royals will chew up anything good in you and spit it out. It's what they do. You're just too stupid to know that."

Dan hadn't been the one to get his head turned by a pretty blonde princess. He wasn't going to point that out to his father, not right now. "We've both kept our distance." *Well, except for*

93

when I kissed him. "Look, Dad, you know Ada is my life right now."

"Why haven't you brought her over to see us then, huh? It's not like we're far away." Tears dripped from his dad's voice.

"We're still assessing the situation. There are some threats, I can't go into them—"

"You're just making this shit up now." Glass shattered on the other end of the line. "I can't believe you. You know how important it is to keep my girl away from those snakes, and you just deliver her up to the enemy like it doesn't even matter."

Dan counted to five. "I'm going to let you clean up your mess. We'll talk when you're sober." He hung up the phone and stared at the wall again. After a few minutes, he called Levi.

"Tell me you've got something. Anything. I'm not picky. I'll do some grunt work on Jamal's case right now."

"Actually, your client's taking a look at that case. He's an interesting guy. Got a law degree for fun because, and I quote, *I was at the school anyway, and I didn't have much of a social life. Why not put the time to productive use?* He does more environmental law than anything else, but he definitely knows his shit. Anyway, I did manage to dig up some stuff

94

that could be relevant to your situation." Levi cleared his throat. "Are you alone?"

"Yeah. My, ah, client is up in his office." Dan steeled himself against the wave of shame. He couldn't identify anything he'd done wrong, so he shouldn't feel the guilt smashing down on him as it was.

"Okay." Levi seemed to hesitate, and then he went on. "So how much do you know about Corvia?"

"More than I care about, less than I probably should. Why?"

"Okay. Corvia's not exactly like the other boys and girls. They're technically a constitutional monarchy, but they're not quite like Britain. The Crown still plays a very active role in politics there. It's not an absolute monarchy, but the king is very much a head of state. Think of it more like Germany in the early twentieth century or maybe like England during the Revolution."

Dan hadn't paid much attention in school. "Wasn't King George a little . . . um, unstable?"

"Yes. Very much so. And so is Sebastian, although I'd say his instability comes from decades of partying too hard and not from an inherited genetic disorder. Sebastian had an arranged marriage with his first wife, she came from an old German aristocratic family. They had three

95

children—Andreas, who will inherit. Selene, the princess royal, and Hans, who's in a heap of legal trouble in Russia right now. And then he dropped his proper, appropriate royal wife for a pretty young thing he met in Dubai."

"That's Eric's mom."

"Right. Well, the marriage didn't work out because they had different ideas of what *conservative* meant. She was not about to put up with the drugs, the mistresses, or the way his children by the first wife treated her or her son. She divorced him—it was a huge scandal. She fled back to her own country, married a man from another wealthy, conservative family, and put the one thing that reminded her of her mistake into boarding schools for the rest of his life."

"Yikes. Sounds—well, I'm not here to judge."

"You are if it creates a security threat. Anyway, she died in a car wreck when Eric was about sixteen. He'd just finished undergrad. She didn't attend graduation. At any rate, Sebastian went on to marry wife number three after the divorce, although it took a while before the scandal died down. That marriage produced three more children, who are currently the darlings of the press for their antics on the European social scene. One of them has made quite a name for herself on the

96

trashier sort of ultranationalist talk show circuit. Another one got drunk and puked into the baptismal font at the Vatican."

"Christ on a crutch." Dan shook his head. "What does any of this have to do with threats to my niece?"

"Directly? Not a lot. I'm still working on that. But you know how this stuff works, Dan. The background details are never irrelevant. Anyway, Sebastian got bored with wife number three and dropped her for actress Carla Tease—"

"Wait—"

"The same star of such grand films as *Blow Him Away*, and I don't mean romantic suspense. He's in his seventies, she's twenty-four, she's given him one son, and they have another one on the way. And she just caught him cheating and made very public objections, for which he—er—*chastened*, is the word local press is using, in public."

"My God." Dan covered his mouth.

"Is nowhere near this scene. While Sebastian's always been kind of a libertine, at least in public, he's been nasty as hell in private."

"Selene said he encouraged them to backstab each other—the kids, I mean. He didn't want to see them cooperating. He thought it was funny when they competed to make each other look bad in front of him."

"She wasn't lying. I found some old media coverage, stills and video, of Selene shoving Eric down the stairs at some kind of state function. He wound up breaking his leg." He cleared his throat. "Eric stopped returning to Corvia when Andreas filmed him in a sex act with another man in Corvia and showed it to their father. It was reported on because Andreas interrupted a staff meeting to show it to his father—and his whole cabinet."

Dan bit down on the inside of his cheek. If he'd known about that when Andreas had come to the house, he'd have decked him, prince or no prince. "That's . . . horrible."

"Of course it is. It's how their father raised them. If his mother hadn't sent him away to schools, Eric would have grown up with that as his normal too. Anyway, Andreas is a bit different from his father. He doesn't have the reputation for partying that his father has. Instead, he's kind of . . . well. He's more of a control freak. He's been slowly moving to consolidate his power in Parliament, and his wife and child never make a peep in the media. They're silent and only ever seen in still pictures."

"That's not ominous at all." Dan shuddered.

"It's possible they may prefer it, especially with the circus following the rest of the family around. I mean, as far as the average person in Corvia knows, both Selene and Eric literally

98

disappeared without a trace. The others are all around puking, partying, and disgracing the Corvian name all over Europe. But I will agree, it's a huge red flag." Levi paused for a moment. "My best guess would be that Andreas wants Ada to come home so that he can give the media something positive, a way to distract from the bad behavior of the rest of the family. He likes things under his control, so it would fit in well under his needs, but that's not likely to be his primary motivation."

"So how do we stop him?" Dan got up and paced. "He's pretty sure Eric's going to jump when he says jump, you know?"

"Eric disagrees." Eric strode into the library and headed straight for the bar.

"Gotta go. Sorry, Levi." Dan hung up.

"I apologize." Eric mixed himself a martini as he spoke. "I didn't mean to end your conversation. I simply wished to assert my position on the matter, since I seemed to play some role in it."

"It's fine." Dan waved the hand that didn't have a glass in it. "I was just chatting with Levi. I had a conversation with my dad tonight and needed a distraction."

Eric nodded once, acknowledging the fact. "Oddly enough, I spoke with my father too." He held up his martini. "Hence the brain bleach."

"Families." Dan forced himself to grin. "Can't live with them, can't shoot them."

"I suppose one can, if one doesn't get caught." He shook his head. "Again, apologies. I've managed to avoid having to speak with mine for years, quite literally. I suppose all of this unexpected contact has me in a darker mood than normal."

"Considering some of the things I just heard about your family, I'm not surprised." Dan glanced away. "I wasn't snooping. It was just because of the whole security situation. You know."

Eric made a face. "Of course. I'm Ada's guardian, so I'm her biggest vulnerability."

"Yeah, I guess that's a way of looking at it. But also, the Corvian royal family is the biggest threat." Dan tugged at his collar. "Don't get me wrong—I'm not saying they'd necessarily hurt her. But they've made it very clear that they want Ada, which is the only clear motive right now. We have to look at it."

Eric heaved a mighty sigh and rolled his eyes to the ceiling, but his whole body had gone stiff. His attitude of supreme nonchalance was a very good act. "Naturally. Leave it to them to make themselves the targets of an investigation without needing to." He shook his head. "Thankfully, I'm long past caring about those days."

Dan knew a lie when he saw one. He didn't know Eric well enough to call him out on the lie, not in a way that wouldn't end in a breach. "Of course." He sipped from his gin and tonic again. "My dad was completely shit-faced," he offered instead. "And then your father called him."

"I'm sure that went swimmingly." Eric sipped from his martini. "Dear old Sebastian just makes friends everywhere he goes these days, doesn't he?" He shook his head. "They've both just lost a child. One would think a man raised to diplomacy could develop the tiniest bit of tact, but no." He bowed his head for a moment. "For what it's worth, I apologize for his behavior. I'd call and offer my condolences myself, but I don't get the impression they'd be welcome."

"It's not personal." Dan managed a little smile. "It's just—well. You know."

"I do." Eric stared into his martini for a moment. "I have a stepbrother in my mother's country. He's going to send some referrals for a nanny—a childcare professional." He swirled the martini around a little. "I hope you'll be willing to help interview her—remotely, of course."

"You're her guardian, Eric. It's your decision."

"Legally, perhaps. We both know you're her real uncle, the one who knew her parents and who knows her. I cannot do this without you."

Dan relaxed. Eric wasn't trying to push him out. "I'll interview them with you, of course. It's part of the security service anyway."

"Of course." Eric smiled again, just a tiny bit, and left.

Chapter Nine

Eric opened his tablet with a groan. Ali's text had come at about two o'clock in the morning, or ten o'clock Ali's time. *Your brother is up to his usual tactics.*

Eric hadn't wanted to look, but the phone's alert noise had woken him. He'd never been the deepest of sleepers, so he hadn't managed to get back to sleep. He'd turned to work to calm himself down, and then he'd gotten distracted by a design for a possible new wind turbine. Now, of course, he felt the lack of sleep, but he was at breakfast and could do nothing about it.

He gratefully accepted the cup of coffee Hadiya gave him and turned to his messages. Ali had indeed followed up his text with another, this time with a link to an article from the most prestigious newspaper in Corvia.

DEATH OF PRINCESS SELENE ELIZABETH MARGARETHE VICTORIA OF CORVIA
The Princess Royal was killed, along with her morganatic American husband, in a car accident in the American city of Boston this week. She is survived by her daughter, Princess Ada (4). His Majesty King Sebastian has decreed the nation shall enter a six-month official mourning period in her memory.

The young princess remains in the United States for now. Her caregiver remains a mystery, although Crown Prince Andreas assures us she is safe in the care of the royal family and will be returned to Corvia "as soon as can be arranged. There are minor legal difficulties to be overcome, of course, as Her Highness passed away without a will. Rest assured that child is the future, and we'll have my niece safely in Corvia where she belongs just as soon as possible."

The editors of this publication have done some research, and we can find no obvious members of the Corvian royal family in the United States. That said, the third son of King Sebastian is known to have studied at university in America and his whereabouts are currently unknown. It is possible he may be the royal in question. If so, this publication strongly approves of his decision to abandon the wildness of his youth and return to Corvia and the responsibilities of his position.

Eric held his head in his hands. He'd only had one drink last night, not enough to lose his many inhibitions, let alone develop a hangover. He

104

shouldn't have this much of a headache at this hour.

Dan gave him a sour look. "You got a second bar somewhere up in that master suite or something?"

Eric shot him a look that should have killed him on the spot, which would have been inconvenient if it had worked. Then he passed the tablet over without a word. Dan was a smart man, and even if he couldn't read the German, he could figure out the gist from the black-framed portrait of Selene.

Dan frowned at the tablet, poked at the screen for a second, and then relaxed. Holding the screen just out of reach, he seemed to be reading it for a moment. " 'The wildness of his youth?' Heh. You make it sound like you were some kind of wallflower when apparently the papers back home saw you as a real wild child."

Eric took the tablet back. Dan had translated the web page into English. Of course he had.

"I'll let you figure out which one was real." He winced as Ada reached for his screen with a greasy hand. "Andreas thinks if he—"

Ada threw her bowl of cereal across the room. "No!"

All three of the adults froze in place. Ada didn't seem to care. Her little face was scarlet, but

105

her pupils were the size of particles found only under powerful microscopes. Her chest heaved as she fought for breath, but it was the only part moving. Eric abandoned his tablet and dropped to his knees in front of her, spilled cereal and milk forgotten.

A little part of him, in the back of his brain, reminded him how ill-suited he was for this. What did he know about a child having a panic attack or a child having a tantrum? He didn't even know the difference.

Ada needed help. It was all Eric needed to know. He got down onto the ground and tried to meet her wide eyes. "Ada, it's your uncle Eric. No one is going to make you go with Andreas. Do you hear me?"

Ada didn't look at him. "I don't like him! I don't want him here!" She screamed as loud as she could, as if volume itself could keep her enemy away.

Dan appeared at Eric's side, close enough for Eric to feel the warmth from his body. Eric shouldn't notice, not at a time like this. He shouldn't even feel it, shouldn't even have thoughts of a sexual nature, not when a child like Ada so clearly needed help. Eric was a truly selfish man.

106

"No one's going to make you see him, love." Dan put a hand on Ada's tiny shoulders, oblivious to the turmoil in Eric's gut. "I'd shoot anyone who tried."

"He will." Ada looked at Dan and regained some of her color, but threw herself into Eric's arms. "He's going to come, and he's going to put me on a plane, and he's going to take me to someplace stupid and make me wear a stupid hat and make me be a princess."

Eric wrapped Ada in his arms. "Ada, you don't have to be anything you don't want to be. Not now, and not ever. I promise you this. As long as I'm alive—"

Ada buried her face in his chest and screamed, vibrations from the sound running straight into his lungs. "You won't be! He'll make you go away just like Mommy and Daddy!"

Eric looked up at Dan, whose eyes had gone wide and solemn. They needed to talk about this, but they needed to do it in private. Right now, the last thing Ada needed was to be left to her own devices. "My love, I'm very used to keeping myself safe. It's why your mother chose me to take care of you, even though we weren't close. But even if *he* gets through *my* defenses, he'd have to deal with your Uncle Dan to get to you. And your Uncle Dan is used to keeping a whole lot of people safe, and he's got so many other people he can call on for help just to keep you safe. You already know how much he loves you, right?"

Ada sniffed, wet and thick. "Yes. But what if *he* gets through all of them?"

"He can't. Your Uncle Dan can call on the whole US Army. And because it's you, he can call on some people from my mother's country too now." Eric didn't know if that was true technically. He hoped it was. Ali had been good to him and had no love for Corvia or the Corvian royals. Besides, Ali loved children. If he saw Ada's terror of Andreas, he'd probably move to take Andreas out on general principle.

"Your Uncle Eric is right, honey." Dan stroked Ada's hair. "We're not going to let him get to you. Sometimes, Eric might have to let him into the house because we like to let the bad guys think they're safer than they are. It's a trick we use sometimes. But you don't have to see him; you don't have to be close to him. I promise. Do you want to go play with your little bowling set?"

It was a bowling set made of soft plush toys, and it had been set up in the formal living room Eric only ever used for company. So far, it was Ada's second-favorite pastime, second only to eating. She agreed to go bowl with Dan, leaving Eric to finish cleaning up after Ada's freak-out.

Once he was done, he moved into his office and called Dr. Omar. The chaplain was surprised to hear from him, but when Eric explained what was going on, he understood right away.

"It absolutely sounds to me like there's more going on there than you're necessarily being told. I won't deny I'm concerned about it."

"I am too, and I think Dan must be as well. He hasn't said anything about a past negative encounter, but it's possible he doesn't know." Eric tilted his chair back and stared at the ceiling, as though two and a half centuries of white paint could somehow bring parenting wisdom forward. "I know I know nothing about parenting. Or about family life, since we're being honest. But if I had a sibling in his line of work and I wanted to keep the peace, I might not tell him about a situation with a happy resolution."

"Of course." Omar paused for a long moment. "My wife, as it happens, is a clinical psychologist. She specializes in work with children who've experienced trauma. I could bring her by to speak with Ada, if you think that would be helpful."

Eric would have sobbed with relief if decades of boarding school hadn't educated demonstrative emotion right out of him. "I admit I was hoping for a recommendation, but I already feel like I've trespassed too much on your goodwill."

"Nonsense. I'm here to help, and if Zeynba found out there was any delay in getting help for a child, I'd be sleeping in the yard. And rightly so. I'll have her reach out with her availability."

"Thank you so much, my friend."

"Anytime."

Eric tried to compose himself for work after he hung up. Yes, there was a problem, and it was one he was ill-equipped to solve. He'd taken the steps necessary to fight the battle. He'd found the help Ada needed. He'd already changed his will to account for the child, to make sure Dan got custody if something happened to him, and to make Ada his heir. Other than that, all he could do was remain open and loving to the child.

Or, at least, as open and as loving as he knew how to be.

As if the thought had summoned more trouble, Eric's phone rang with a video conference request from Andreas.

He could refuse it. Eric had that kind of power. He could simply decline the request and move on with his life. He had no obligation to sit around and spend time listening to his asshole brother. At the same time, it didn't take a genius to

110

know he had to keep the lines of communication open.

"Good morning, Andreas." He managed a polite smile for his half brother and hoped he didn't expect anything more.

Andreas' laugh was cold, affected. "Good lord, brother. You look terrible. I suppose my niece kept you up all night. It's a pity. You certainly aren't going to tempt that wretched soldier into your bed looking like *that*."

Eric ground his teeth. If Andreas were here, Eric would have a hard time not punching him. Getting emotional had never helped him though. Instead, he just rolled his eyes. "I'm not trying to tempt anyone into my bed, Andreas, and least of all, Selene's brother-in-law."

"Of course you are. Anyone with eyes could see the way you looked at him, pathetic puppy that you are. I suppose he's exactly your type though. You always did want a knight in shining armor to rescue you from your ivory tower."

Eric had to laugh. "The only thing I ever needed to be rescued from was my family, and I've managed to avoid you all for more than ten years without any kind of knight, thank you."

"But you'd take one if one presented itself, wouldn't you? And who could blame you? He's handsome, fit. Heroic. Women have always thrown themselves at him, or so Selene told me at that dreadful wedding. You should have been there— oh, wait. You weren't welcome." Andreas' grin mocked him from the screen. "Of course, you're paying him to stick around. He wouldn't spare you a second glance if it weren't for your money."

The words landed like a punch, but Eric had endured many over the years. He didn't react visibly. "This happens to be a point on which I was previously informed, thank you. This is how things work when one hires a person. Is there a reason you called, Andreas? I'm aware how fond you are of the sound of your own voice, but even you must find yourself tedious by now."

Andreas chuckled. "I was wondering how well you liked my article in *Corvia Journal-Gazette* this morning. I'm sure your gift subscription must have kicked in by now."

"Cancel it. Don't waste taxpayer money. It's a tabloid, and I've never made time to read them." He waved a hand. "Interesting wording though. You make my youth sound much more exciting than it actually was. Since when has the crown prince needed to get a job as a hack writer though? I know the days when idle royals had value are long gone, but the treasury seems to disagree."

"Ah, little brother. Perhaps I'm simply taking a page from your book. Just because I have the option to be idle doesn't mean I'm choosing to be idle. Now is the time for all children of Corvia to return to their roots, don't you think? The princess belongs here, an example for all. Bringing hope to her people."

"Her parents thought otherwise." Eric yawned. "At any rate, if you're done, I'm desperate for a nap. Ava is an active little girl, and adjusting to the energy level of a preschooler has been an adventure."

"It doesn't matter how much beauty sleep you get, little brother. Daniel Marshall will never want a Corvian royal to begin with. He only tolerates your company now because of your pocketbook."

"Goodbye, brother." Eric terminated the chat.

Andreas was an asshole, but that wasn't news. He wanted to get his hands on Ada, but that wasn't news either. Eric wasn't even surprised to find Andreas trying to intimidate him into giving up Ada.

He still couldn't understand why Andreas was trying to lure him back to Corvia, when neither he nor Selene had any other goal during their childhoods other than chasing him out. And why Andreas would want to meddle in Eric's love life, other than to ruin it, was anyone's guess.

Chapter Ten

Dan made himself smile as Dr. Zeynba Omar, wife of Eric's chaplain friend, made herself comfortable in one of the superfluous sitting areas of Eric's house. This one was a little less formal than others, but the curtains had been drawn against anyone with a telephoto lens so it looked ten times stuffier than it actually was.

"Are you going to be okay in here?" he asked Ada. The little girl was wrapped around her favorite teddy bear, a much-loved old thing that could probably use a good wash. Dan didn't want to be the one to try to pry it away from her for now.

"Will you and Uncle Eric be near?"

"We'll be close enough to hear if you scream, but not so close to listen when you talk to Dr. Zeynba. It's important for you to feel safe telling her anything—even if you wouldn't want to say it to one of us. Understand?" He kissed the top of her head.

"Okay." She took a deep breath. "I love you."

"I love you too, sugar. And remember—she's married to sweet Dr. Omar, Uncle Eric's friend who's been so nice and helping us all out. Right?"

Ada relaxed a little and gave Dr. Zeynba a little smile. "I like him. We can do this."

Dan managed to relax while he left the room. Then he went to find Eric, who was sitting in the next room with his phone in his hand. The books on the shelf beside him had already been reorganized, this time in height order.

"I thought we were going to review anyone who came into contact with the kid. For security."

Eric bowed his head. "I know. I'm sorry. I thought it was important to make arrangements for help for her as soon as possible. My plan was to run it by you as soon as Ada had nap time, and then my brother called and everything went out the window. To include, apparently, my common sense and basic manners. I apologize."

Dan shook his head and sat down. "You don't make it easy to get pissed at you, I'll say that much." He sighed and pulled out his own phone, already sending a text to Ben.

He hit send before he remembered that Ben wouldn't respond. *Damn it.*

116

Eric gave him a moment. "People manage. My intent was to get recommendations for a psychologist, but when it turned out that Dr. Zeynba was already in the field, it seemed like the best solution. Dr. Omar is already familiar with our situation, so it's safe to assume she would be too." He managed a wry grin. "He's kept my secret at work, at the very least."

"That's something." Dan ran a hand through his short hair. "So, about that. Um, I don't have the right to take Ada out of your sight, and I feel kind of weird about that anyway. But, um. My dad and mom want to see her."

Eric blinked. "Well, my home is yours as long as you need it to be. You certainly don't need to ask to invite people over, for any reason. I trust you not to bring people in who'd be a threat to Ada." He swallowed, and Dan tried not to stare. "I mean, she's your family too."

Dan bit down on the inside of his cheek. "Well, my parents aren't exactly comfortable with . . . um. They'd rather I bring Ada to see them. And while the thought of taking Ada out of the house is giving me hives, I also kind of see their point. Selene and Ben wanted Ada to grow up knowing what normal was. They didn't want her thinking everyone lived in a palace, you know?"

Eric raised an eyebrow. "This is not a palace, Dan. But I'm not going to try to stop you. There's no one better equipped to keep her safe than you are."

Dan stared into Eric's eyes. He couldn't find any deception. "Are you for real right now?"

"I'm always for real. We both agree you're the one who's best suited for her care." Eric waved a dismissive hand. "I'll always defer to you when it comes to decisions about her—her safety, her health, whatever. When it comes to matters of law or of science or of any of the languages I speak, I'll expect deference in return. I am not the expert on children, on security, or on family. Part of being smart is knowing when to stay in my lane, as it were." He twisted his lips into something resembling a smile.

Something inside Dan's chest snapped, like an old rubber band. "Come with us."

Eric huffed a little. "From what little I know of your family, that would be a disaster."

"Well, I won't pretend Mom and Dad will be thrilled about the decision. Selene's family didn't make the best impression on them." Dan blushed and cleared his throat. "On us. I can admit that. But, Eric, you're part of this kid's life now. You're also local. They need to accept that if they want to stay in their grandkid's life, you're part of the package."

118

He reached out and put his hand on Eric's shoulder. He wanted more, but this wasn't the right time or place. Maybe he should be grateful for the pint-sized chaperone. He shouldn't want Eric anyway.

"And they should get to know that you're actually a good guy. The family in Corvia might be—not to their tastes," he amended, rather than calling them the trash they were. "I may not know you well, but I've gotten to see you under pressure for the past few days. You're a good man. I'd say you're more of a prince than any of them, but I'm afraid you might take that as an insult."

Eric's laugh sounded a little strained to Dan's ears, but at least he tried. "You might know me too well. Thank you, at any rate. I appreciate your support. If you want me to go with you, I will. Just tell me when."

"Tomorrow, maybe?" Dan didn't want to have time to get cold feet.

"Excellent. I'll be ready." His phone buzzed with an incoming notification, and he glanced down and made a face. "Excuse me for a moment. One of my undergrads just got into a spot of trouble with their local police over some equipment. I need to make some calls and sort this out." He slipped away, already dialing the number.

Dan was not prepared for the jolt of need that lanced through him. He wanted to be the focus of Eric's attention. He could see himself running his hand through those dark curls even now. Did his hair feel soft and silky, like it looked? There was only one way to find out.

He banished the thought by pulling out his phone and pretending to check a message. Eric was hot, and he was sweet too. He was smart, and he had a heart of gold. He was everything Dan wanted in a man, but he was also a prince. And Dan would rather chew off his own leg than tie himself to that family.

Not that Dan had any business thinking about tying himself to any families at this point in his life. His job essentially took him all over the country. He stayed in one role long enough to get the job done, and then he transitioned out. Maybe that was why Ben had gone along with Selene's insane idea to give Ada to a brother she loathed — Dan didn't have a stable enough lifestyle to offer her.

Or maybe everything was exactly what the lawyer had told them, and they'd done it for the reason they'd given.

"Are you quite all right?" Eric peered at him, lips pressed together. "Should I call for an ambulance?"

120

"Huh? What?" Dan shook his head. "Sorry. Got lost thinking about something, that's all."

Eric sat back. His phone was nowhere to be seen. "Yes, well. Grief can take us all in strange ways. When you were unresponsive for several minutes I was concerned about a stroke, but—"

"Several minutes?" Maybe Dan should go back to Colorado. He didn't want to leave Ada, but Eric was getting under his skin in ways he couldn't afford.

"Just as I said."

Ada ran into the room and kissed her uncles. "Is it all right if I go upstairs?"

"Sure thing, sweetheart. Would you like me to put you to bed?" Eric rose. "It's probably late enough."

"Okay, Uncle Eric." She hugged and kissed Dan, and then led Eric over to the stairs.

Dan turned to Dr. Zeynba as soon as the rest of them were out of earshot. "Look, I understand there's an issue of patient confidentiality here, but I'm responsible for Ada's security. Is there anything we should be concerned about from Andreas?"

Zeynba sat down stiffly, like she'd just overdone it at the gym. "You have to understand, children's memories are fragile, Mr. Marshall. It's one of the reasons using hypnosis and 'recovered' memories is so dangerous in court. We're seeing things through the eyes of a child here who has, in general, been very sheltered and very well protected. That's a good thing—she's four. She should be sheltered. She should be protected.

"There's only one gap in that, and the gap is with this Andreas. There may have been an incident, I don't know exactly what happened. It does sound like an abduction, but if it was, she was very small. I'd say maybe three years old. Were you informed of anything a year ago?"

Dan stretched his mind back. "I'd just joined Five Star, after recovering from an injury. I was working a job protecting a bank in Iraq against a specific threat. I was pretty out of the loop on a lot of things back here. I know Ben said we had a lot to catch up on, but Ada was like moss on a rock when I got back. Would not let go." He chuckled. "I had to come and stay with them when I got back because she'd only leave Selene's side if I was there."

"It's that fear again. Her fear of this Andreas is all consuming, and I have no real reason to think it's irrational. It doesn't necessarily mean her uncle wants to harm her. My husband isn't trying to spread secrets around, but he did tell me about Ada's mother's background so I'd know what I was walking into.

"Andreas may truly believe he has her best interests at heart, but he's not acting in a child-centered way. If he tried to take Ada by force, or in a way that felt to her like it was forceful, even for a visit that she didn't know about, she'd be beyond terrified."

"If we were forced to go to court . . ." He took a deep breath. "I don't think we would be because Selene's will was very specific. Eric's the lawyer though. If we had to go to court, would you say sending her back to Corvia was in her best interests?"

Zeynba shook her head. "For one thing, there is no *back* to Corvia. She doesn't speak German. She was born here. She's completely removed from Corvian traditions. She might adapt eventually, but her fear of Andreas is such that it would be too traumatic for her to have contact with him or for him to have custody of her."

"Thanks, Doctor. I hate to bring you all the way out here like this, but I'm sure you can see why we were so worried."

Zeynba smiled softly at him. "Mr. Marshall, I can only admire fathers who show such concern for their children's mental health. I meet so many parents who wave things off, or who say *she's just looking for attention*. It's refreshing to see people smart enough and loving enough to take a

123

demonstration like that seriously. Yes, she's also grieving the loss of her parents and traumatized by the sudden change of everything she's ever known. But you're doing the absolute right thing by calling in help when you need it."

Dan blushed. "I mean—we're not fathers. We're just uncles. On opposite sides."

Zeynba covered her mouth with her hand. "Oh—my apologies. The way Ada spoke about you, she made it sound like the two of you are partnered up in a more permanent way. A more long-term parenting kind of thing."

Dan forced a smile. "Don't worry about it. I can see why. Thanks again."

Zeynba all but fled. Dan knew he should comfort her, but he was too embarrassed himself. He couldn't shake the image of a nice little family unit from his mind.

But Eric didn't understand family. What if Dan could be the one to teach him?

Chapter Eleven

Eric used extra antiperspirant as he prepared for the first family outing. He didn't know why the idea of this whole thing made him so nervous. He knew why it *should* make him nervous. Here in the house, he knew all of the entrances and exits. He knew how an enemy was likely to try to gain entry, and he knew where he could hide Ada until the threat was dealt with. Out in the wild, things were different.

But that wasn't what had his sweat glands working overtime. Eric might not know Dan's service record personally, but he'd done his research. He knew a man couldn't get into the Rangers or stay in the Rangers without being a supremely competent warrior. Ali had dealt with Five Star Security before and could vouch for the fact that the company didn't hire people who were anything less than stellar examples of their profession, both in terms of physical and mental prowess. If Dan couldn't keep Ada safe, no one could, and so Eric could turn his brain to other issues.

If he were to pause for a moment of self-reflection—say, in the shower before leaving for the familial visit—Eric would have to admit he knew exactly why he was so anxious about the visit. Eric had met the family of exactly one of his former partners. Said partner had dropped him like a hot rock the day after the encounter.

None of his other relationships had gone so far. In fact, Eric had broken up with one boyfriend (a delightful young man by the name of Michael) when he'd put his foot down and insisted.

Dan was not Eric's boyfriend. Dan would never be Eric's boyfriend, so it wasn't logical for Eric to fear meeting his family this much. Dan was someone who shared responsibility for the child under Eric's care—not family, not a friend. He'd kissed Eric once out of pity, and that was all. The sooner Eric pushed that kiss out of his memory, the sooner he'd be able to act like a normal human being again.

He dressed decently, although not as formally as he might have under other circumstances. He wanted to show respect. After all, Theodore Marshall had just lost his son. He still had Dan, but Dan made it sound as if their

126

relationship was somewhat strained. It wasn't Eric's business and he'd stand by Dan from what little he knew, but it was still important to show respect to a person grieving such a loss.

He also didn't want to overdress. From what he'd heard from Dan, it wouldn't go over well.

When he arrived downstairs, he realized he'd missed the mark entirely.

"Christ, don't you own jeans? It's an afternoon get-together, not a faculty cocktail party."

Hadiya glowered at Dan. "Dr. Alawi dresses as he sees fit. And, no, he doesn't own jeans."

Eric's face burned. Even his scalp got hot under his mop of curls. "Perhaps it's best for you to take Ada yourself. I don't want to leave you to deal with everything on your own, but the last thing I want to do is to give offense."

Dan just shook his head. "How do you get to be thirty and not own a pair of jeans?"

"I'll let you know when I turn thirty." Eric straightened himself up. He couldn't show his discomfort. It would be too much. "Are we quite ready to leave? Is there anything I should bring? A bottle of whiskey, perhaps?"

Dan sniffed. "The old man would probably like that, but he's been hitting the bottle hard enough. Let's just go."

Eric grabbed an unopened bottle of bourbon from the bar on his way out the door. He couldn't show up empty-handed.

He'd gotten the vehicle Levi recommended, right down to the child safety seats. He'd ordered it in different colors both for the interior and exterior. It should feel familiar enough to Ada for her to be comfortable, but not so familiar as to remind her of the night she'd lost her parents. She hesitated to get into the SUV, but after a moment, she climbed up and settled into her safety seat.

Dan drove. Eric was capable of driving, of course, but he didn't do it often. Dan knew where they were going, and if anything went wrong, he had the training to get them out of any hostile situations. All Eric had to do was sit and fret from Cambridge to South Boston.

The Marshall family lived on Sixth Street, in half of a bright-yellow duplex that seemed to be a beacon to paparazzi and assassins. It even had a black wreath on the door, a sign of mourning for Ben. Eric chastised himself for the uncharitable thought. These were normal people who didn't go through their days like they were living in a spy thriller. They had a right to mourn like anyone else.

He and Dan each took one of Ada's hands and climbed the stairs before Dan rang the doorbell. Eric still had time. He could run. If Ada were with

128

Dan, no one would come for Eric. He was under no illusions as to his draw for Andreas, if Ada weren't in his custody.

The door creaked open. Theodore Marshall stood an inch or two shorter than his son. A few strands of red remained in his white hair. Sorrow, along with whatever else life had given him, had etched deep grooves into his cheeks. He wore jeans and a plaid shirt.

Ada threw her arms around him. "Grandpa!"

Tears leaked freely down the furrows in the older man's cheeks. "My little sunshine, my Ada! Has that bad man been keeping you from me?"

Eric stepped back down the wooden stairs. He didn't turn around, that would be too dramatic and draw too much attention. Instead, he just backed away as quietly as he could.

Ada stamped her little foot and put her hands on her hips. "Uncle Eric is not a bad man, Grandpa! He's good. He helps me and he's good to me, even though I yelled at him and even though I threw my cereal. Even though I got scared. You have to be nice to him."

Eric stopped and reached out to stroke Ada's hair. It wasn't far, after all. Everything down here in South Boston was cramped, so even though he'd made it down to the sidewalk he could still reach.

"It's okay, sweetheart. Your grandpa can feel however he needs to feel about me. His heart hurts just like yours does."

Theodore curled his lip and turned to Dan. "You had to bring *him* with you?"

Eric turned his gaze to Dan. "I only came along to help manage things on the way." He shifted his gaze to Dan. "Send me a text when you're ready to leave, and I'll be back."

Dan rolled his eyes. "I'm not going to leave you to wander the streets of Southie on your own, man. Come on, stick around. It'll be fine."

The venom dripping from Theodore's expression told Eric nothing would actually be fine, but he was on the spot here. "If you're certain."

Dan set his jaw and turned to his father. "Eric stays or all of us go."

Theodore turned his back and stalked into the house. He looked a little unsteady on his feet, but stayed upright as he made his way indoors. Ada hugged Eric and skipped along inside.

Dan grinned at him. "That went better than expected." He gestured. "After you."

The Marshall family home was neat and tidy and smelled a little bit like yesterday's cabbage. Dan's mother emerged from the kitchen to embrace Ada and give her son a cool smile. She trailed her eyes over Eric. "So this is the child thief?"

130

Eric ground his teeth but stayed silent.

Dan did not. "Actually, he's the one both Selene *and Ben* decided was best equipped to keep Ada out of the hands of the rest of those freaks. I wasn't thrilled about it at first, but knowing what I know now, I agree with them. I'm not going into it in front of Ada. She's too little."

"I'm four!" Ada gaped at Dan in outrage. "I'm not little, I'm big!"

"You are big in so many ways." Eric smiled at her and put a hand on her shoulder. "But there are some things you don't need to hear about yet because they'll only scare you. It's not much fun to be scared, and when you've got your Uncle Dan to keep you nice and safe, you don't *need* to be scared. Right?"

Ada scowled, because even at four, it must have seemed like a spurious argument. "Well, you did promise me I wouldn't have to see Mommy's bad brother again, so okay." She turned to Mary Ann. "Can I come see what you're doing in the kitchen? Uncle Eric has a kitchen, but Miss Hadiya says it's not safe for small girls."

Mary Ann sniffed. "How else are you going to learn to cook for yourself? I swear, people these days." She glared at Eric and held out a hand. "Come along. You can sit and watch while I finish up our lunches."

131

She led the little girl into what looked like it had to be a very cramped kitchen and abandoned the living room, her husband, Eric, and Dan.

"So." Theodore glared at Eric again. "Are you sleeping with him?"

"Oh, for the love of Christ." Dan rolled his eyes so hard his whole head got into the act. "There's a guy involved, so you think I must be having sex with him. Do you sleep with every woman you meet? No? Then what in the name of Jesus and all his saints makes you think I'm dropping trou for every dude who walks by? Open up a goddamn book."

Eric bit down on his tongue. He had nothing to add that could be helpful.

"He's a prince. He's used to getting his way. You don't think for a minute I'm buying that phony security business, do you?" Eric hadn't noticed the full glass of whiskey next to Theodore's seat, but now he saw it shake as Theodore lifted it to his lips.

"I am, technically, a prince." Eric stiffened. "I haven't associated with anyone from my father's side of the family, or that country, since I was fifteen. I'm not going to convince you of anything, and that's fine, but I can promise you, I was just as surprised as your son when I found out about the terms of Selene's and Ben's wills. Right now, it seems as though breaking the will is not in Ada's interest. When the current situation stabilizes and Ada is safer, I'm happy to revisit custody arrangements."

"You'd give her up just like that?" Theodore recoiled. Even Dan gave Eric a weird look. "You really are a piece of work, ain't you?"

Eric rolled his eyes to the sky and prayed to a god he didn't really believe in to give him patience. "It isn't my needs or desires that matter. It's hers. Ada is the one whose psyche needs the most care right now. I will *only* do what is right for this girl, and alienating her from the family who loves and cares for her is hardly in Ada's best interests. Dan is the superior guardian because he knows her. I'm just a man who shares a small amount of DNA with her. I love her, I care for her, but I'm not what she needs. Dan is."

Theodore stared at him as tears rolled down his cheeks. "Then why did that bitch leave her to you instead of him?"

Dan let out a little growl. "*That bitch* is her mother, thank you."

Eric put his free hand on Dan's arm. "He's angry, and he's right to be. It's a little misdirected, perhaps. I couldn't say exactly why. Selene and I loathed each other. I didn't even know she was in Boston, or that she had a child. Or that she'd gotten married. From what I'm told, it's my success at

133

avoiding the rest of our family and the paparazzi that led both her and Ben to choose me. I have certain other advantages as well, if they should become necessary, when it comes to keeping Ada out of Corvian hands. And I will use them, if forced. I'd prefer not to take her out of the area where you live because I may not have much experience with families but I know they're important."

Theodore stared at Eric's hand on Dan's arm until Eric removed it.

"I'm having a lot of trouble believing you'd just hand her over like that." Theodore snapped his fingers. "But maybe I've got a bias against you. I don't have a lot of good feelings about your country. And you came here with Daniel, and he and I haven't ever seen eye to eye on a damn thing.

"But I did just see you with Ada. She's the light of my life, and she trusts you like I've never seen her love or trust anyone before. So I'll tell you this, Mr. Fancy. I still don't like you. I still don't trust you. But I do think you at least *think* you've got that girl's best interests at heart."

Chapter Twelve

Ada had a great time playing at Grandma and Grandpa's place. They ate grilled cheese and bacon on the tiny backyard patio while she happily explained how she liked Hadiya's cooking but never got bacon at Uncle Eric's house. They played so much Candyland and Chutes and Ladders that Dan was sure he was starting to see candy canes flashing before his eyes. And Mary Ann played dress-up with Ada until darkness fell.

Dan wouldn't describe his own time with his parents in such rosy terms. After Ted provoked a fight with Eric, embarrassing him and their whole family, Dan had wished the ground would just open up and swallow him whole. There was a reason he hadn't come back to Boston during his leave time, after all. He'd gone out to California while Ben was at Cal Tech, and to all the other places Ben had worked. After Ben married Selene and settled down, he'd stayed with them.

His parents never invited him back, and he never asked.

Ted mocked Dan's work ethic. He belittled Dan's intelligence. He sneered at Dan for his sexuality and for his lack of "family loyalty." Dan didn't even know what that was supposed to mean, but whatever. It all kind of blended into a constant drone of negativity that he just couldn't escape.

It was like Ted woke up, looked at a bottle of whiskey, and asked it how he could best make Dan look like an ass.

Poor Eric, though, had it worse. As near as Dan could tell, he wasn't an observant Muslim, since his bar was pretty damn well stocked and he clearly drank from it. Evidently, he still didn't eat pork though, because he declined the grilled-cheese-and-bacon sandwiches. Ted and Mary Ann somehow knew Eric wasn't eating pork, because they shared an absolutely savage grin between them when they saw his empty plate. They took every opportunity to get their digs in, and Eric accepted it all with the stoicism of a freaking Vulcan.

Of course he did. Dan had met his family. Hell, he probably thought Dan's parents were the kindest people he'd ever met, poor guy.

Dan almost kissed the sidewalk when they finally made their escape. He held it together and didn't say anything in front of Ada though. He even managed to keep his face pleasant and relaxed until they got her settled into bed. Then he staggered downstairs, at odds and ends.

He wasn't sure what he needed or what he wanted. He knew hiding in his room would be the absolute worst thing for himself. Still, while this wasn't his house, he couldn't exactly call himself a guest. It wasn't anyone's job to entertain or soothe him.

The last thing he expected was to find Eric waiting for him in the library with two martinis. He handed one to Dan and raised the other one in a kind of toast. "I thought you could use something." He looked away, cheeks slightly pink. "I don't know. Sorry. I know it's foolish."

Something inside Dan melted. He sat down on the sofa, leaving plenty of room for Eric to join him. "You probably need it more than I do. They were deliberately mean. I'm so sorry—my parents decided to put their entire asses out on display tonight."

Eric sat gingerly on the edge of the sofa, like he was the guest. "Well, I did make one of these for myself. But, Dan, they couldn't really do much to me. They didn't have any power over me."

Dan stared at Eric. He knew Eric had been speaking English, in that snooty, upper-crust

London drawl of his that used to drive him batshit insane. "That doesn't make any sense."

"Sorry. I cared about them, of course, but I knew they were lashing out partly because they blame my family for losing Ben. And they're right. If they wanted to be rude, fine. If they want to blame me for Selene and Ben's decision, that's fine too. They've lost a child. There's nothing worse, at least for parents who have souls. They can't actually hurt me. They can't do anything to get the child away and they don't have anything to give to Andreas, so it only bothers me in terms of how they treated you. Which, I must say, was difficult to see."

Dan looked away. "It's nothing, really. They're kind of . . . um. They're old-fashioned, I was kind of rebellious. They were pissed when I stopped going to church. They were more pissed when I came out. Dad marched me right down to the Army recruiter and signed me up then and there." He sipped from his drink. "They love Ada though."

"There's no doubt of that." Eric let out a long slow breath. "If you want them to come over, it's not a problem. I mean it. I do want you to consider this as your home while you're here, for as long as you need it."

Dan stared at him for a moment. "Sometimes, I wonder if you're real."

138

Eric huffed out a little laugh. "I'm real. And I do mean it. Ada is what's important. This house is easy to defend. It was built for defense. If it comes right down to it, you can keep the house and I'll find someplace else after we've dealt with the threat."

Dan scoffed. "Come on."

Eric just smiled softly. "I don't want to argue. I just need you to know I'm not what your family thinks. I'm not like them."

Dan didn't have to ask to know what he meant. "I know you're not. I'm not sure how you got this way, but I'm glad you did."

Eric's blush deepened. "You're too kind."

Dan put his drink down. He'd already made his choice, committed to his action, whether he intended to or not. He never made time for self-doubt once he committed. Later, maybe, once the action was done and he had time to examine his successes and failures, but for now, he had to act.

He leaned forward and brushed Eric's smooth cheek with his fingertips. When Eric turned, startled, Dan leaned in and claimed Eric's mouth with his.

Eric didn't hesitate to accept him. He opened his mouth to Dan and welcomed him, letting Dan taste and explore. Juniper and vermouth tantalized just a little bit—he'd barely touched his martini.

He moaned as Dan pulled him closer. Dan needed more. He could feel Eric warming up underneath all that fancy clothing; he needed to feel even more. He needed the scent of him, the taste of him. He needed everything.

Why would you, when you're just going to leave?

Dan ignored the little voice in the back of his head, the one that sounded suspiciously like his conscience, and pulled back for air. "Was that okay?"

Eric's pupils had widened with lust already, and his lips twisted into a wry grin. "I'd say it was more than okay. But, Dan, you don't want this—"

"I do, actually. I want this more than I have words to say."

He could see shadows behind Eric's dark eyes, but Eric didn't give them a voice. He bit his lip, just a little bit, and nodded. "Upstairs though. Where we have some privacy."

Dan had no problem complying. He stood and held his hand out. Eric allowed him to help him up, and Dan led him up the stairs to the second floor.

They crept silently past Ada's room toward the master suite. They hadn't talked about a destination, but simply made their way there. Dan didn't know what he expected to see, but he didn't register anything other than the king-sized four-poster bed.

He closed and locked the door behind them because the last thing either of them needed was a tiny person seeking relief right now. When he turned around, Eric had already found lube and condoms and placed them on the nightstand. "Not to be presumptuous," he said hastily. "I just like to be prepared."

Dan closed on him in an instant, licking his way back into Eric's mouth while stripping that ridiculous sport coat off him. "Be presumptuous. It's okay." He worked on Eric's button-down shirt as he spoke. "I like it."

Eric didn't waste a minute peeling away Dan's shirt. He even stood back for a moment, drinking Dan in, and hell, if Dan didn't love it. Most of his hookups were furtive things, in the dark, and no one wanted to see those scars anyway. Eric didn't shrink away, and it hadn't occurred to Dan that he might. He could stand there and bask in Eric's admiration, wallow in it.

"I know I'm not going to be the only one getting naked here." He grinned over at Eric, hand on the top button of his jeans.

Eric divested himself of his clothes without fanfare, folding each item quickly and placing it on a chair. He never looked away from Dan, and the

141

heat of his gaze was like an aphrodisiac of its own. Dan could almost believe this could be more than a hookup.

Eric was beautiful. He didn't have the kind of muscle Dan was used to, but he wasn't a military guy either. Eric had long lean muscles, an elegant body, the body of a man who kept himself in shape but didn't live in the gym. He held his head high, still not looking away from Dan.

Dan never did figure out who broke the moment first. All he knew was they were suddenly in the big bed, and he was on top of Eric, and everything was right with the world. Everything about Eric was just right for him, lined up perfectly. Their tongues slid against each other, his body spread out on the crisp pale sheets.

And Eric responded so beautifully to Dan's touch, it was like he'd been made just for Dan by whatever god looked after gay former soldiers. He didn't need to posture and try to pull more from Dan or create some kind of weird one-upmanship. He was just content to give Dan what he had to offer, and accept what Dan had to give.

He opened readily for Dan, tight but eager, and for half a second, Dan knew doubt. Eric wasn't some jarhead he'd met in a bar near base somewhere. Dan wanted to give him everything, but he didn't know if he could be as gentle or as

142

tender as Eric needed. Eric wasn't some delicate flower, but he also wasn't used to the kind of rough, almost-just-died sex Dan knew. And while Dan didn't care about hurting any other member of the Corvian royal family, he didn't want to hurt Eric any more than he wanted to hurt his niece.

But Eric reached for him and wrapped his long legs around Dan's waist. Dan would be whatever Eric needed. They were both adults, grown-ass men who could speak for themselves and ask for what they needed. He rolled the condom on, slicked himself up, and worked his way inside.

"Holy crap." Dan held himself still as long as he could while Eric adjusted. He wasn't the smallest guy, and he knew it would be a second. The intoxicating combination of being inside of Eric—of Eric taking him in, accepting him, making space in his very body for him—and the sweet friction of the sex act itself combined to drive out most of his higher functions. All he could do was stare down at the miraculous man beneath him, waiting for the word.

"Move, please." Eric's voice was low, as if he could possibly wake the others in this cavernous house. Dan could hear the strain underneath anyway. He knew how to give Eric what he needed.

He snapped his hips back and drove himself in again, and then again as the tension melted from Eric's face. Bliss took its place as Dan grazed over his sweet spot, over and over again. He let out a little moan before he grabbed a pillow, giving full voice to his pleasure.

That wouldn't do. Dan wanted to hear everything. He wanted to see Eric lose control. He wanted to hear what Eric sounded like when he hit nirvana, when the world and its troubles faded away if only for a few seconds. He wanted to see his face too, and the pillow could only interfere.

But the pillow was wise, and necessary. As Dan's thrusts became stronger and Eric's cries more uninhibited, Dan realized the risk of waking the kid was real. The last thing they needed—any of them—was a case of coitus interruptus.

As he sensed his orgasm sneaking up on him, he took hold of Eric's thick strong cock and stroked it in time to his thrusts. Eric didn't need much to send him over the edge, and the force of his orgasm brought Dan along behind.

He staggered into the bathroom to get rid of the condom and to grab something to clean them both up. He kissed Eric tenderly, tucked him into bed, and then sneaked out the door and back to his own room.

144

He regretted leaving as soon as the door closed behind him. No, he wasn't ready to explain anything to Ada yet, but they could have set an alarm or something. Anything to hold Eric in his arms for just a little longer.

Then again, maybe not. Eric hadn't asked him to stay, and neither of them had any illusions about this being a permanent arrangement. Maybe it was best not to give themselves a false sense of security.

Chapter Thirteen

Eric woke up with the kind of delicious soreness that came from a good workout. It would have been ideal had he also woken up in a slightly less empty bed, but Eric had been under no illusions on that count. Men like Dan did not stay the night with men like Eric. Men like Dan sought out other stunning model types, other soldiers, or men who could give them what they needed.

They did not seek out men "with the emotional capacity of the average table lamp," to quote a former partner. At least, they didn't seek out men like Eric for more than an hour or two.

Well, an hour or two had done Eric a world of good. He'd take more, but he was more than content with what he'd gotten too. He washed up and started to dress, just in time for Ada to wake.

Should he relax his standards and wear the T-shirt and sweats? Dan had commented on them, had spent some time looking at Eric the one day he'd tried it.

No. It would be pathetic. One night, however good, did not mean Eric needed to go changing his life around — especially when he knew nothing would come of it. He dressed in something approximating business casual and hurried to get a start on the day.

By the time he got downstairs to eat, Ada and Dan were awake too. Ada wasn't exactly a morning person. On the contrary, she tended toward grogginess for several hours no matter what time she woke. In the schools to which Eric had been consigned, she would have been forced to wake up several hours earlier than everyone else just so she could learn to adjust to their schedule.

Eric vowed to himself that Ada would never go to boarding school, no matter who had custody of her in the long term.

"So what is it we plan on doing today?" he asked the rest of the family as Hadiya entered the kitchen. "I'm hoping to get some work done on a new geothermal energy project, but I can take some time to play—"

He stopped when his phone rang. He recognized the number right away. His attorneys rarely bothered him, so when they did, it was a big deal. "Hello, this is Dr. Alawi."

"Dr. Alawi, this is Kristin Ainsley. I hate to bother you so early in the day, but I was hoping we could discuss the situation with your niece's custody."

Ainsley's voice was crisp and professional, but the hairs on the back of Eric's neck stood up. He got up and retreated to his office, passing the metaphorical torch to Dan. If he let his hand brush against Dan's on the way past, well, surely Dan would interpret it as an accident.

"Of course," he said as he retreated to his private space. "I can only assume there have been new developments, given the call."

"Of course, sir. Two lawsuits have been filed by parties seeking to obtain custody of Ada."

Eric doubled his speed. "That's interesting. I can guess who one of the parties is."

"His Royal Highness Prince Andreas has filed suit contesting the will and custody on the grounds that the will would be invalid in Corvia and based on your 'immoral' lifestyle. Ordinarily, I'd say this would be laughed out of court, given that this is Massachusetts, but his position carries weight and the State Department might throw their weight into the mix. We are preparing our defense, but I'll assume you'll want to review everything."

"Of course." He heaved a sigh. "I suppose this means my days of anonymity are about to be in short supply."

"It depends on how nasty your brother chooses to get, but lawsuits there's always a risk of the lawsuit going public and a certain type of journalist does tend to flock to anything that even vaguely suggests royalty. We've petitioned the court to seal all documents and proceedings, but we'll see what happens. His Highness could choose to leak the information anyway—it isn't as though the courts could do anything to him if he did, other than perhaps expelling him."

Eric kept his outward composure as he sank into his desk chair. No one could see him in his office with the door closed, but he didn't want to build up sloppy habits. He couldn't hide the sudden pain in his gut. "Valid. I'll notify Five Star, and we'll address the situation. Who is the other plaintiff?"

"Theodore and Mary Ann Marshall, Ada's grandparents. They filed the suit first thing yesterday morning."

Eric sucked in his cheeks and glared at the door, not that it was going to do much good. "I was just at their home yesterday. They didn't choose to mention it."

"I'm not sure how they would have brought it up. 'Thanks for coming by. By the way, we're suing you for custody and child support.' It doesn't exactly have a welcoming ring to it."

Eric sighed. "It might have been more welcoming than my actual reception. It would at least have been honest." Ainsley wasn't calling to hear him whine about his personal life. She was calling to update him about important legal matters, and Eric was paying her in fifteen-minute increments. "Ada isn't a bargaining chip, and she isn't to be treated as such. Visits stop until Theodore gets treatment for his mental health and his alcoholism, no unsupervised visits at all."

Ainsley paused. "Dr. Alawi, are you certain you want to push back in that way here? By the time this works its way through family court, you should have dealt with the other matter and Ada will be with her uncle. It's your money, of course, and you're welcome to do as you wish with it, but I question the necessity of fighting on three fronts right now."

Eric hadn't realized he'd made a fist. He stared at it and forced himself to relax. Ainsley was a brilliant lawyer and was only doing her job. "I can't take the risk that the grandparents will get custody either. Their behavior toward Dan is vicious and cruel. I need to demonstrate that my

151

concern for Ada extends beyond keeping her out of Corvian hands. I would not be surprised to find out that Andreas has a file on every drop Theodore has ever consumed and every DUI he's ever dodged."

"Excellent point. I hadn't considered that. As for the other matter—are you certain you want to surrender Ada to her other uncle? And the house? Florian can still put the documents into a safe place, and not file them."

"I am. I can always find another home for me and Hadiya, and Dan is the better choice. A man should know his strengths, and where he has room for improvement. I am not a family man. I love that girl. I would dearly love to be what she needs, but I wouldn't even know where to start."

"And your sister's poison pill?"

"Andreas will reveal everything anyway." Eric turned to look at the window, only to find the heavy curtains shut.

"Even the—er, the recording?"

Eric's face burned. "He'll find some way to release it. At which point, everyone involved gets arrested. Fifteen isn't even the legal age of consent in Corvia, never mind the United States. They can't arrest Andreas, but we'll bankrupt every media outlet that shows it." His stomach threatened mutiny, but he forced it into submission. "I can't change the past, but I can absolutely affect the present. Are we ready to do what we have to?"

"We are on our end. It . . ." She took a deep breath. "I've been on the business end of revenge porn myself, sir. It was hard. Even though I had the law on my side, the repercussions are still coming down to this day. I'm aware that you're . . ." She hesitated, and her tone shifted.

"I know you're smart, Eric. I know you're a genius. I'm not speaking as your lawyer here, but as someone who's gotten to know you about as well as anyone over the years. I care about what happens to you, I've been through some of this myself, and I just want to make sure you're a hundred percent making an informed choice here."

Eric managed to smile, just a little. "Thank you, Ms. Ainsley. I appreciate your concern. I know this won't be fun or easy. I expect it will be humiliating. I expect I'll lose my position at the university.

"Fortunately, I don't rely on my income from that job. If I'm forced to do so, I can take my money and go to Canada or France, perhaps. There are options. But I will not sacrifice this child to whatever Andreas is plotting or to my own shame."

Ainsley sniffed. "You're a good man, Eric." She recovered most of the professional distance in her voice. "The firm will do everything in our

153

power to prevent the worst-case scenario, of course. Florian and I will keep you posted."

"Thank you. I'll speak with you soon."

Eric closed his eyes and bowed his head. He hadn't wanted to think about that stupid recording. He'd been a fool. He should have known no one was going to be interested in him for his own sake, and certainly not someone like Max. Being fifteen was no excuse. If something seemed too good to be true, it usually was, and Eric's greatest sin had been in forgetting that.

He couldn't let himself sit here in the dark and mourn though. He was a grown man with a life, and while it might not be the kind of life most people thought of when they thought of royalty, it was one he enjoyed. More than that—he had a child depending on him now, plus Hadiya. He needed to pull himself together and get himself back on track.

Someone knocked on the door. "Come in," he said without thinking.

Dan opened the door and frowned before turning the light on. "I didn't think you had enough to drink to be hungover." He walked over to the desk. "You okay?"

Eric forced a smile. "Just a call from the lawyers." He sighed and sat up straighter. "Did you know your parents have filed suit against me for custody and child support?"

154

Dan curled his lip. "You're joking."

"I only wish I was. They filed it yesterday morning, before we showed up at their house."

"Goddamn it." Dan all but fell into the chair on the other side of the desk. "I had no idea. They never said anything. I'm so sorry—they had no right to do that. I swear, we aren't money-grubbers."

Eric shook his head, a wry grin on his face. He had yet to meet the person who wasn't after his money, at least once they found out who his father was. Dan was the first, but he was also unique. "They have every right to want to keep Ada out of Corvia, and to ask for money to help maintain her. I told the attorneys to file a countersuit eliminating visits until Theodore gets treatment for his mental health and alcoholism."

Dan jumped up. "That's not okay."

Eric raised an eyebrow. "They're citing my lack of moral character as grounds for removing Ada from my custody, and my insistence on him getting treatment is what isn't okay?"

Dan deflated a bit. "I'm sorry. It's—he's complicated. He does need the help, it's just—it's not okay to use Ada as a weapon to make that happen."

"I'm not." Eric stood up too. "When this is all over, you'll have full custody of Ada, Dan. I

155

don't trust Theodore, after what I saw, not to try to get her from you too. Of course you'll want her to visit with her grandparents, and I'd be a monster if I objected to that.

"But I'm also not going to encourage her to go into an environment where you're being denigrated by someone who isn't able to control himself, even for Ada's sake. You'll be her sole guardian, Dan, not the cool uncle anymore."

Dan blinked a few times as he processed what Eric had just told him. "Wait—you're serious. What about what Selene said in the will?"

"The lawyer asked me the same thing. Andreas has filed a lawsuit for the same reasons. I'm fairly certain neither you nor anyone else is going to want me near any children after everything comes out in the wash. Don't worry—you'll be provided for, Ada will have whatever she needs."

Dan looked around the room, like he was looking for a hidden camera. "What's going on here, Eric? Do you have a secret life of crime you want to tell me about or something?"

"Or something." Eric managed a smile and retreated to his bedroom.

Dan didn't follow.

Chapter Fourteen

Dan had to wait until nap time, when Ada was safe in her bed (and a certain small redhead who was too smart for her own good was asleep and couldn't eavesdrop), to reach out to someone. It wasn't that he didn't trust Eric. He trusted Eric implicitly, which was a hell of a lot more than he should, all things considered.

That was why he needed the outside voice. Someone had to act as the external, thinking brain.

The first number he dialed, of course, belonged to Ben. Ben always knew what to do, how to help. *Hi, this is Ben. I can't get to the phone right now—*

Dan choked off a curse, hung up, and dialed Levi.

Levi sounded like he'd been hit by a truck when Dan caught him, but he said nothing was wrong. "Jamal's client's case got wrapped up finally. Things were a little dicey there by the end, but it looks like everything's officially worked out, plus, we're getting a long-term contract for the company out of the deal. I'm glad I could be part of it actually. What's going on with you?"

Dan fought against the urge to apologize and hang up. He hadn't gotten as far as he had by pushing his problems off on other people.

At the same time, this was about so much more than just Dan or just the Marshalls. It wasn't even about Dan and Eric. This involved international politics and a tiny little soul who just happened to be an excuse. "Things are getting weird, from a legal perspective." He explained what was going on, his alarm over Eric rising as he heard the situation described in his own voice.

Levi made a disgruntled sound, kind of like an off-key hum. "Well, I mean, we do have attorneys but, frankly, Prince Eric's—"

"Don't ever let him hear you call him that." Dan glanced around on the off chance that Eric might be in the room. The guy moved like a cat sometimes. Dan could never be sure he wasn't right around the corner.

"Right. Sorry. I've been picking up some chatter. Dr. Alawi can afford better lawyers, and has them. For that matter, he *is* a better lawyer. As a hobby. Which is weird." He yawned. "Sorry. Late night. Anyway, I'd say the courtroom drama isn't part of our scope of operations, except what he said at the end there has me kind of nervous."

"Do you have any idea what he could be talking about? I'm sure you've run some kind of background on the guy."

"The only thing I can think of is the video his brother used to out him to his father. From what I can see, Eric hasn't been back to his mother's country since the video aired either. It looks like he's actually a political asylee, as near as I can tell." Levi cleared his throat. "Which is something I suspect he doesn't share often, but here we are."

"Why would he think no one would want him around Ada because someone videoed him without his consent?" Dan blinked. "That doesn't make sense."

"Probably because he became a man without a country before he even turned sixteen because of it. He's seen the media. A royal sex tape? They'd be all over it. It's an issue for sure. Even if you get a judge who doesn't have a bias against gay men, the issue of media presence is going to come up. Which is exactly why Andreas would release that tape."

Dan's stomach turned. "He's going to blackmail his own brother into sending Ada into hell."

"And Selene blackmailed him—with the same threat, even if it was unstated—into taking

Ada in the first place." Levi sighed. "The poor guy can't win, and he's smart enough to know it. The question is, what can you or Five Star do about it? And I'm not sure there's an answer."

"Are we sure the tape is still out there?"

"Oh yeah. Andreas doesn't let anything go if he thinks it could be useful later on. And he's not stupid enough to have thought Eric would have just disappeared and never resurfaced." Levi paused, and Dan heard clacking in the background. "In other news, I've heard from the feds investigating the crash that killed Selene and Ben. Ordinarily, I wouldn't, but these feds happen to be guys I know. Agent Gomes—who lives with the head of Mass State Police Major Crimes unit, in case you were concerned about local knowledge—said there's data from the cell towers in the area they can use, but it's going to take time to tease it out. 'Like getting gum out of an eight-year-old's hair,' he said, and I don't even want to know how a guy like him knows that."

Dan didn't want to know either. "Sounds terrible, actually. So we've got nothing."

"Oh, on the contrary. We're certain it's murder. We can prove it's murder. We just need to prove who did it. That's all." Levi chuckled softly. "Hey—don't worry about Ada. He's already made provisions for her."

160

"That's not it, okay? It's—I know. He told me." Dan closed his eyes. "I'm worried about him."

Levi went quiet for a long moment. "I can see why you might get attached. He's a prince—"

"He's a guy. He's a traumatized guy who opened his heart and home to the daughter of a woman who despised him, okay? And I lit into him on sight, just because of his family, and he still opened his home to me. For Ada. He didn't hold my behavior against me because he knew I was grieving even if he couldn't feel the same way. He's a damn good man, Levi. Let's just leave the Crown out of it."

Levi laughed. "Never did think you'd fall for someone, Dan."

"I haven't."

"Have too. But look, I'd make sure he knows sooner rather than later. Stuff's going to come to a head soon, and he's going to make his decisions his way. He's not used to having backup."

Dan opened his mouth to object, but the sound of the doorbell interrupted him. "Damn it. I'd better go before Prince Independent decides to do it. Thanks, Levi." Dan was already running toward the stairs.

He had his gun out by the time he got to the front door, which he only opened a crack. Somehow, he wasn't surprised to see Andreas

161

there, flanked by his guards from Diplomatic Security. One corner of Andreas' mouth twisted upwards into a smirk. "Aren't you going to invite me in, Marshall?"

Dan snorted. "Not without Eric's permission, and I know damn well he didn't invite you."

Andreas scoffed. "I have nothing to say to him right now that can't be said through our attorneys. It's unfortunate that he forced me to go to such extremes, but he always was a foolish boy. I'd hoped he'd learned wisdom with time, but at this point, he's too old for me to coddle his juvenile impulses. He needs to learn that the rules apply to him too, and that his parentage doesn't exempt him from the law.

"No, Marshall, I came all this way to visit with you. Now let me in so we can discuss business like men."

Dan considered for only half a second. Eric would be livid if he let Andreas into the house. He'd made a promise to Ada, after all. He didn't want to let Andreas go without hearing what he had to say though. Not only would that antagonize Andreas without cause, but Andreas was likely to say something incriminating if Dan just let him blather.

He stepped outside and closed the door behind himself. "We can talk out here. Apparently, letting Ada see you is bad for her mental health." He tossed Andreas his best eat-shit grin.

One of the guards twitched, like he was trying not to laugh.

Andreas rolled his eyes and heaved the loudest sigh Dan had ever heard. "So dramatic. I'd expect nothing less from Eric, of course. He was always a drama queen. I'm surprised to see a Ranger going along with it. Your kind were always supposed to be manlier than that."

"When it comes to traumatized children, I'll go with the folks who have the alphabet soup after their names. We brought in an actual psychologist. Apparently, little Ada's got some issues she needs to work out, and a lot of them seem to center around you. Can't imagine why that would be."

"Hm. She'll learn her role soon enough. I'm not surprised she's fighting it so hard, considering Selene's behavior before her marriage. So much rebellion. So much disobedience. It's disgraceful. I'm sure an Army man like yourself can understand my position."

Dan let that one slide. The only person Andreas had ever served was himself.

"I couldn't help but notice your use of the word *we*, Marshall. You seem to think my brother

163

sees you as an equal—almost as a co-parent. You even brought him back to South Boston to meet your parents, didn't you?"

Dan stared at him for a moment, just long enough to convey his disgust. "You spend an awful lot of time thinking about where your brother goes and what he does, considering how much you hate him."

"On the contrary, Mr. Marshall. I don't hate him. That's precisely what's at issue here. I am the crown prince of Corvia. I have a responsibility—to our traditions, to our people, to our laws, to my father. That responsibility governs how I must behave. Eric also has a responsibility, one he's shirked for over a decade. He understands his place. You are a commoner. You could never understand exactly why concepts such as love and hate are completely irrelevant here."

Dan rolled his eyes and leaned against the doorframe. It looked casual, but he had access to both of his guns. "Well, you don't get much more common than me. Which begs the question—why are you here?"

"To spare you, idiot. When I saw that you'd actually brought my brother to meet your parents, I knew I had to intervene. I'm not a cruel man, whatever you may have heard. I understand there may have been some indiscretions. You're grieving, he's more than available, he has power and money, you're cooped up in the house all the time—but my dear boy, that doesn't create a relationship and it never can."

Dan's hands and feet went cold. He hadn't been thinking of a relationship. He hadn't been consciously trying to avoid one either, although he knew he didn't want one with someone in this rat pit of a family. "Shouldn't a crown prince have better things to do with his time than make shit up about other people's sex lives? It seems like something a tabloid reporter would do, not someone who's supposed to be at a trade summit."

He decided to show just a tiny bit of his hand. "Of course, there isn't a trade summit happening. So maybe you've got more free time than you expected."

Something flared behind Andreas' icy eyes, but his voice was no less restrained than it had been before. "It's adorable how you rush to his defense. It's also pathetic, but it's adorable. You know he wouldn't do the same for you, of course."

"Well, considering that my brother is dead, and not here menacing someone he thinks is sleeping with me, Eric probably wouldn't be forced into this position." Dan pursed his lips. "Did you have a point?"

165

Andreas yawned, but it didn't look real. It looked fake, affected. "If you must be so gauche about it, yes. I realize you may have formed an attachment to my brother, but don't get attached. Not that you could. No one ever does. He's a whore, you see. He spreads his legs for whoever will have him. It's how he's always been, since he was a teenager, and you certainly can't think *you* would be the one to make him settle down.

"Believe me. I know. The man is a prince. You're the help. If none of the hundreds of men between fifteen and now have been enough to satisfy him, you certainly aren't going to do the job. And Eric, for all of his many terrible qualities, knows his job quite well. He's to provide the Crown with another heir. He's to take his place in the government. And he will do it—he will return to Corvia and do as he's told. A hireling like you may be enough for a brief fling, depending on your attributes, but you could never tempt him away from his duties."

Andreas' words were like an oil slick. Dan couldn't outrun them, and he couldn't swim past them without being coated by them. He could fake it though. "Buddy, you're seriously barking up the wrong tree here. Eric and I aren't worried about any kind of relationship that doesn't relate to Ada. She's literally our only concern. We ain't thinking about

166

some kind of love nest or whatever your deranged brain is dreaming up, and we're not spending our time mooning around.

"He came to my parents' place for Ada's sake, not for some kind of weird dating ritual. Get over yourself. And don't ever—and I do mean ever—let me hear you referring to that man as a whore again, you got that? I don't care if he's been with one man or a thousand, it's not for you or for anyone else to pass judgment on."

Andreas laughed, low and dark and dirty. "Of course. I see how it is. I simply wished to spare you the inevitable heartbreak, but I see you're as stubborn as your brother. You'll soon find out the truth—but I've done my duty. Farewell."

"See you in court." Dan turned around and went back into the house. His footsteps echoed in the empty vestibule.

Chapter Fifteen

Eric spun the wheel and jumped his marker the requisite number of spaces. He didn't understand the rules of this game, or why it focused so completely on sweets, but it seemed to make Ada happy. She didn't ask to have the sweets pictured in the game. She just wanted to play this inane game with mountains made from wretched gumdrops.

Eric didn't have to understand. He just had to accept.

"The bad man came to the house yesterday while I was having a nap." Ada spun the wheel. "Uncle Dan said you didn't know."

Eric only hid his surprise through decades of practice. "Uncle Dan is telling the truth. He hadn't told me." He glanced over at Dan, who sat on the sofa scrolling through his phone. "Should I inform the attorneys or no?"

Dan grimaced. "Er, probably? He wasn't here to see you, I guess. He was giving me a hard time, trying to run me off." His cheeks turned a deep shade of red, almost magenta, and Eric didn't need to know in what way he was trying to run Dan off.

"I see." Eric held back a sigh. "I'm sorry you had to go through that. You're certainly not being paid enough to have to put up with him."

Dan flinched, with his whole body. "Is that how you see me?" His voice was soft, wounded. "Someone you hired?"

Eric bit his lip. Facts were facts, after all. He had hired Dan—but not for the reasons Andreas probably thought, or insinuated. "I hired you because I didn't want your employer to stop paying you while you tried to sort things out with Ada." He met Dan's eyes. "I *see you* as Ada's rightful guardian. I see you as a brilliant and brave man who shouldn't have any facet of his life affected by Corvian messes. Andreas doesn't know me well enough to tell you how I see anyone, never mind how I see you."

Dan gave him a sad little smile. "Sorry. I know I shouldn't let that guy get to me."

"It's difficult not to. Andreas has spent forty years honing his personality into a weapon. He

170

knows how to hurt. It's what he does best. He enjoys it."

Ada climbed into his lap. "I don't like him."

"No one does, sweetheart." He kissed the side of her head.

"That's sad. Maybe that's why he's so nasty." She shrugged. "As long as I have you two, though, he can't get to me."

"That's right, Rabbit." Dan winked at her.

Eric forced a smile. He'd already gotten too attached to Ada, much to his own shock. He shouldn't have let himself do it. He needed to pull back before everything blew up and he had to leave. "I've heard from the attorneys on a related matter. Apparently, the press back in Corvia is clamoring for photos of Ada."

"Nothing doing." Dan folded his arms over his chest. His jaw jutted out a bit. He probably didn't realize he was even doing it.

Eric hesitated. The last thing he wanted was to override Ada's real uncle, but this was one area in which he knew what he was talking about. He hugged Ada a little bit closer. "I'll admit that the idea of a family portrait to satisfy the curiosity of a nation on another continent, which has brought me about as much joy as oral surgery without anesthetic, isn't high on my list of good opportunities right now."

171

"Good. We're on the same page." Dan stood up.

Eric sighed. "However." He only had to raise his voice a little bit.

Dan turned around with a pained look on his face. "Ugh. What?"

"However, giving them a photo that we've controlled and selected will kill demand for paparazzi pictures. Obviously, I'd have to word the agreement correctly, but I can do that in my sleep, and it's a good way to minimize the number of disgusting people trying to peep in our windows."

Dan curled his lip, but then he sat down and bowed his head. "I hate that you know that. But you're probably right. I just—where could we possibly do it? I don't want them in your house."

"It's your house too, Dan. It'll be your house entirely soon enough." Eric pushed back his irritation at the way Dan kept ignoring that fact.

Although maybe he didn't want the old house. Maybe he planned to pick Ada up and move them out to Colorado. What did Eric know? He had no right to so much as ask. "Anyway," he continued as smoothly as he could, "we can do it at the university. It's easy enough to shut down a section for something picturesque. Students do it all the time."

Dan made a face. "I hate it. I hate it from a security standpoint, and I hate it from a fuss and bother standpoint. But you're right—it probably is the best way to get rid of the paparazzi issue." He rubbed at his face. "It just bugs me—we haven't even buried Selene and Ben, but here we are doing photo spreads of Ada."

"I know." Eric didn't know. He wouldn't have been welcome at either funeral. He wouldn't have been able to let Ada go either because they weren't going anywhere near either family without him. But he could make the right sounds and try to give Dan some comfort. "If there were a better way, we would take it."

Eric was able to arrange space in one of the Harvard art museums, since it would be easiest to secure, and the matter was settled. He trusted his attorneys to ensure the event remained closed to other members of the royal family currently in the United States—specifically, to Andreas. He'd made Ada a promise, and he intended to keep it.

When they got to the museum the next day, therefore, Eric was mostly shocked to find his brother's entourage in front.

He left Dan in the car to guard Ada. He couldn't leave her by herself, after all, and Andreas wouldn't do anything in public. Eric had been very specific in his arrangements with the Corvian

173

photographers, with Harvard security, and with the Cambridge Police. Anything they did would be done in public.

Andreas, of course, was dressed to the nines. He had his full court costume, with actual *medals* pinned to it, and an actual cape. He looked ridiculous. "You look like you've just stepped off the stage of *Hamilton*, and not as one of the good guys." Eric looked his brother up and down. "Go home, Andreas. There's nothing for you here."

Eric was aware of the cameras. There were tourists all around—it was Harvard, there were always tourists, and at this time of day, some of them were even sober. There were reporters too. If Andreas hadn't been the one to invite them, Eric would eat his own shoes.

"Of course there is. There's a family portrait being taken. I'm here as part of the family. Stand aside, *brother*. You have no authority here." Andreas curled his lip.

Eric rolled his eyes. "I'm the one who reserved the space, I'm the actual staff member, so I'm the only one with authority here. Ada doesn't want to see you. She doesn't have to see you. Now leave."

Andreas waved his hand, dismissive as ever, but his face darkened to pink. "I'm a prince. I'm going to be king. I'm not bound by the whims of a

174

child, who probably still wets the bed at night. She'll have to see me on a regular basis when we bring her back to Corvia to take up her rightful place as princess."

"She's not going to Corvia. There are plenty of people with a better claim to custody than you have, Andreas. Look, the photographers have a limited amount of time. I'm sure you'd rather be respectful of their time than show your contempt." Eric didn't dare risk looking directly at any of the media people. He had to trust them to know his meaning.

Andreas scoffed. "I've given them what they wanted for years. You've been hiding here like a coward. Which one of us disrespects them again? If you want to show your great love and respect for them, start the session."

"Andreas, you are not included in this portrait."

"I am the prince. I am your future sovereign, and you will do as I tell you!" Andreas backhanded Eric.

Eric could have blocked. Hell, he could have broken Andreas' elbow if he wanted to. Andreas never expected people to fight back, and he left himself wide open. If Eric had defended himself, the men from diplomatic protection would have been forced to intervene, and not on Eric's behalf.

175

As it was, they stood back and watched tourists and the media snap plenty of pictures of Andreas hitting Eric.

And of Cambridge police stepping between Andreas and Eric. "That'll be about enough of that." The sergeant in charge of the event was a large barrel-chested Black man. Even Andreas had to back away a little bit. "You need to leave. You might be a prince wherever you came from, but around here, that's assault."

"He's got diplomatic immunity." The taller guard from diplomatic protection sounded sheepish.

"That just means I can't stick his ass in jail. It doesn't mean he gets to go around assaulting Cambridge residents. Get him out of here, or I do it for you."

The diplomatic protection agents didn't need to be told twice. They ushered Andreas off the property quickly, without any of the gentleness he probably thought he deserved. And at least a hundred cameras caught every minute of it.

Eric thought he'd feel a little bit of triumph. After all, he'd just goaded Andreas into humiliating himself on camera. Instead, he just felt hollow and a little empty where Andreas had slapped him. He paused for a moment and then returned to the car.

176

"All right, let's get this show on the road." He reached into the vehicle took Ada's hand.

Dan hopped out of the other door. Ada took his hand once he circled around to her side, wide-eyed and shy at the sight of so many interested people. "Did the police take him away?"

"They did." Eric smiled at her with an ease he didn't feel. "They absolutely did. Would you like to meet the sergeant who helped?"

And so the photographers got plenty of pictures of sweet Princess Ada thanking the big strong policeman who'd run off the wicked prince. Eric could just see the captions now. To be honest, he couldn't have invented a better narrative if he wanted to poison public opinion against Andreas. It hadn't been his intention, but he wasn't going to turn his nose up when a gift fell into his lap.

The media got plenty of pictures of the two uncles holding the princess. It was funny how posing for the cameras, without looking like he was being deliberate, came back to Eric. He'd thought he'd shed all of those habits when he took his mother's name, but he supposed it was a lot like riding a bicycle. Royalty should always expect to be on camera, should always be ready to be seen.

It was a lesson he'd learned the worst way possible, but here he was.

177

Dan had grumbled about having to wear a suit to this photo shoot, but he reluctantly admitted that Eric had been right. The official photographers insisted he stay in the shots, and Eric wouldn't have let him escape even if they hadn't. It was vital to all of Eric's plans that Dan be seen with Ada, that his niece be forever linked with this amazing man and her father's side of the family both in public opinion and in fact.

He knew with each click of the shutter that his own privacy, his own anonymity, was fading away. Soon, everything would come out into the light, his every misstep and his every shame. He'd miss Ada. She'd wormed her way into his heart in such a short time.

He'd miss Dan.

This was the way it would have to be though. No one was going to save him. No one was going to intervene and make everything okay. Eric had started over before, and he would do it again. Every time was painful, and this would be no different—except in one way.

This time, he was taking Andreas down with him.

178

Chapter Sixteen

Dan knew there would be fallout from the public stunt. The fact that one of the leading online gossip sites had video posted before they even got home from the shoot boggled Dan's mind, but he couldn't say anything in front of Ada. Ada was upset enough at having seen Andreas hit Eric.

"He hurt you!" She turned to Dan with a mask of rage on her tiny face. "You let him hit Uncle Eric!"

Dan squirmed under her vitriol. He couldn't pretend she wasn't right. He'd been hired to protect Eric. He *wanted* to protect Eric. Andreas' attack was like a knife to Dan's gut. How could he sit by and let someone hurt this incredible man?

Eric, bruised cheek standing out like red paint on a white wall, got down to her level. "Ada, I know it looks bad. But there are two things to remember. All right?" He held up one slender finger as she nodded, solemnly.

"First, Dan's first responsibility is to you. Not to me. I'm a grown adult and you're a child. *Every* adult has a responsibility to defend children before they defend adults, do you understand? It's not just Uncle Dan. I'm not mad at him for it—in fact, I like him more because he kept you safe."

Ada pursed her lips and glared at Dan again, but she nodded. "You said two things."

Eric laughed. "I did, my dear. If Andreas was focused on me, he couldn't focus on you. I knew there would be an argument. I pushed him to get angry so he wouldn't think about where you were. It's not the first time he's hit me. I was expecting it. I did it so he would get angry and leave you alone. Do you understand?"

Ada bit her lip. "No. I don't like to get hit. At playgroup the teachers make you sit in a corner, even if you're the one who got hit instead of the one who did the hitting."

"Well, that's wrong too. I did it because Andreas likes people to think he's a very controlled and very put-together guy. You and me, we know the truth. And with all of those cameras, all of those people watching, now a lot more people know the truth. He's going to try to say I'm not the right person to take care of you. What he did today proves he's not the right person to take care of you either—and there are a hundred people who saw it."

Her eyes widened. Dan could almost see the synapses connecting in her brain. "So he can't tell the teacher you lied."

"Right." Eric smiled and ruffled her hair. "Do you need help changing into something more comfortable, or do you want to play in your dress?"

"I'll ask Hadiya." She beamed at him. "I think you and Uncle Dan want to talk."

Dan's face burned. He hadn't realized a four-year-old would pick up on things so easily, but Ada had always been a smart kid.

"Let me get an ice pack for that." Dan gave Eric's cheek a pointed stare. "If we're going to be dealing with cameras, you want to minimize the bruising as much as possible."

"On the contrary. After what Andreas just did, I think I want to let the world see it for as long as it lasts." Eric followed him into the library anyway. "Thank you for staying with Ada. I know it can't have been easy."

Dan threw himself onto the couch. "Are you kidding me? If it weren't for her, I'd have broken the bastard's neck. He didn't have the right to put his hands on you." He glared at the door. "No one does."

Eric's cheeks turned pink. "You're too kind."

Dan turned his body so he was fully facing Eric. "Look, I know things are weird. Our situation is weird. I'm not . . . I'm not the guy who's going to just dine and dash, okay? I'm not sure where anything's going, but that doesn't mean I'm okay with some Neanderthal, who thinks he's someone, smacking you around. You're important, Eric. You're important to Ada. You're important to your students. And you're important to me, honestly."

Color faded from Eric's face. "You don't mean that, Dan."

"Actually I do." Under ordinary circumstances, Dan would have been annoyed by the contradiction. He was pretty sure he understood why Eric didn't believe him. "Like I said, I don't know where anything's going. Right now, I don't have to. I just know you matter, okay?"

Eric looked away, face red. It was okay. Dan didn't expect him to answer. He knew no one had said anything like that to him before. They had other things on their minds right now anyway.

The awful gossip rag might have been the first to run with the story, but they weren't the only one. Eric's boss at the university called an hour after they got home, absolutely incensed that reporters had called him to get his reaction to having a prince on the payroll. Dan could only hear one side of that conversation, and even that was muffled as Eric

182

took it from his office. It didn't sound like fun though.

Reporters called them directly. They called Eric. They called Dan. They called Hadiya. Dan could only assume they'd gotten their numbers from Andreas, although how *he'd* gotten them was a mystery. Dan turned everyone's phone off, with his set so only Levi could get through.

"I'm responsible for your safety, right? That means mental safety too. No one needs this kind of harassment."

Eric set up an autoresponder for his emails that would direct people to his attorneys. It didn't stop anyone, but Dan hadn't expected it to. He just wished Eric could get some peace.

He put up signs around the property as well, conscious of the reporters filming him as he did so. If the film crews and increased traffic bothered the neighbors, none of them seemed inclined to poke their heads out and say something. Maybe they understood—they all must have paid a good sum for their places so close to Harvard too. Money came with certain risks, and one of those risks was celebrity.

At least the signs Dan put up reminded them to stay off the property. They weren't allowed to ring the doorbell or try to get pictures through the windows—not that the windows were open, not since the paparazzo incident.

Finally, the end of the day came. Eric and Dan got Ada to bed and sat with Hadiya to watch the news, filled with a morbid desire to see how bad the damage was. They chose a reasonably staid local channel for their exercise in masochism, but even that proved to be a hazardous undertaking.

The anchorwoman was normally one of those wide-eyed, understanding types. Now though, she bubbled over with excitement. "We've always been proud of the wide range of people who've chosen to call Boston home, but today we learned we've had a handsome prince right here in Cambridge. Prince Eric of Corvia, third son of King Sebastian and fourth in line for the throne, has been disguised as a mild-mannered professor of environmental science and policy at Harvard University for the past five years."

The screen behind her changed to the confrontation with Andreas.

Dan looked away. "At least they picked up on the messaging you wanted."

Eric shuddered. "Their writer should be taken out and flogged. Didn't they have a revolution—and start it right here in Boston—so they wouldn't have to get so breathless about

184

royalty?" He reached for the remote and turned off the television.

Dan pretended he didn't notice how Eric's hand trembled. "All right. Well, I'm ready to call it a night." He stood and stretched. "How about you, Eric?"

Eric nodded, and then he hauled himself to his feet. "I suppose we should be well rested for whatever storm hits us tomorrow." He looked down and away. "If there's one good part about all this publicity, it's that it's happening now. I don't have to go back to work until September, assuming I still have a job. By then, the students will have long since forgotten about me. They'll be on to whatever nonsense the government has dreamed up or the latest celebrity screwup or some other nonsense."

Dan had to chuckle. "Yeah, they might be. I have to say though, you're pretty unforgettable."

They'd reached the top of the stairs now. Eric turned to face him, eyes shining with something Dan couldn't identify. It was a good look on him though. Dan couldn't look away.

"You can't say things like that, Dan." Eric's voice was a low rumble, velvet over steel.

"I can if I mean them." Dan took Eric's hand and pulled him closer. For half a second, he thought Eric was going to resist.

Then Eric cradled Dan's face in his hands and kissed him like he could draw Dan's soul from his body. Dan staggered back until he hit the wall. Eric was thinner than he was, but Dan hadn't been ready for the onslaught. Not that he was complaining—if Eric wanted his soul, Dan would hand it over with a smile.

He fumbled for his door and tried to guide Eric into his room, still trying to keep himself upright. His pulse raced in his ears, but only in the best way as his blood rushed south. He managed not to fall until they hit the bed, by which point it didn't matter.

"Forgive me." Eric was breathless, eyes wild with need and something else. Sure, there was lust. Dan had felt Eric's lust poking into his thigh when Eric grabbed him. There was something else there though, something Dan hadn't seen before.

Something Eric hadn't let him see before.

He stroked Eric's face with his hand. "There's nothing to forgive. I like knowing you want me. I like knowing you're into it. It makes me feel good." He stood up and started unbuttoning Eric's shirt. "You could be with any guy you wanted, but you're choosing to be here with me right now. That means a lot."

Eric huffed out a little sound; it might have been a laugh. "I don't want anyone else. I don't feel

186

comfortable—I don't feel like this with anyone else." He glanced around and shrugged out of his shirt, then went to close the door. "You shouldn't have to put up with it."

Dan unbuttoned Eric's trousers and helped him get rid of them, shucking his underwear along with them. "I'm not putting up with squat, Eric. I told you before. I care about you. And I think you care about me too. It's not a hardship to give you something we both want." He nipped along Eric's bare collarbone.

Eric made quick work of Dan's clothes, and Dan got them both into the bed. Eric presented himself for Dan, head down and ass up, and Dan had to admit there was a lot about the sight before him that appealed to him. He rubbed his hand on the globes of Eric's ass in appreciation, and he took advantage to reach for the lube.

"Eric, is this really how you want it? Because we can do this however, but I've got to say. I like to see you. I liked watching you come the other night and I want to see you come again." He worked Eric open as he spoke, listening carefully for the little sounds of pleasure Eric made as Dan worked his way into his body. "You going to let me do that? You going to ride me so I can see everything on your face?"

Eric's breath hitched. "You'd want that?"

187

"Hell yeah." Dan grinned, even though Eric wasn't looking at him. "I want to look right at you the whole time. See that long body of yours."

Eric took a deep breath. The next thing Dan knew, Eric had rolled them over. His dark eyes had a wicked glint to them, and he was reaching over to the nightstand for the condoms. "Anything you want."

Eric rolled the condom onto Dan, and then he lowered himself down onto Dan's cock so slowly it was like he was deliberately tormenting him. And then—then he bottomed out, fully seated and so tight, so hot, eyes burning like two coals in his perfect face. Dan wondered if the world would just stop, then and there—

But it didn't. Eric gave himself time to adjust and then worked up to a rhythm that astounded Dan. He'd never have expected such intensity from someone who showed so much reserve—but he wasn't going to turn it down either. He thrust up to meet Eric, determined not to be outdone, but that only made Eric work harder.

Neither of them lasted long. Dan's orgasm exploded through him. He took Eric's stiff, hot cock in hand and brought him off in only a few seconds, like he needed only a tiny bit of touch to release whatever he'd been holding back.

And then it was over. He collapsed in a sweaty heap, panting, and then gently dismounted. "Thank you for that." He held onto the edge of the footboard. "That was incredible."

"You could stay." Dan swallowed. "If you wanted."

Eric hesitated. Then he nodded, slowly. "I shouldn't—Ada, and all. But yes."

Chapter Seventeen

The video hit the very next day. Eric wished he could say he was surprised. He might not have grown up around Andreas, but he'd spent enough time in his company growing up to know his patterns. He was a genius, after all, even if he didn't like to use the term. He knew exactly what to expect from his brother.

And because he knew what to expect from Andreas, he and his legal team had a plan in place. The first release appeared on one of the more popular homemade porn sites at five o'clock in the morning, Eastern time. The injunction hit said site at 5:02.

Eric might have wished he was surprised by what his brother had done. Since he couldn't be surprised, he was ready.

Of course, the fact that the full force of every anti–child pornography law in the world was being directed against that particular video didn't mean

191

no one had seen it. By the time Eric got out of bed at eight, it had been viewed ten million times, and that was only the number of views counted on legal sites. His name—and an image of himself as a teenager, with anything "obscene" carefully blurred out—was on the front page of every news site and every paper in the world.

Back when this had been new, grief and despair had been the primary emotions Eric had to cope with. Shame ran a close second, and that one had never really gone away. It had been so easy for him to get taken in, and here he was supposed to be a genius. He deserved every bit of scorn and ridicule he got.

Getting kicked out of the two countries in which he'd held citizenship? That barely registered.

Now things were different. The shame was still there, suffusing his whole being, but it warred for position with rage. Oh, he understood why Andreas decided to sink so low. He even understood why Andreas thought he had the right, even if he didn't agree. How Andreas thought he could get away with it *here*, in a country without princes, lay well outside the realm of his understanding.

When the video first made its appearance, back when Eric had been a teenager, suicide had been an option. If he were being honest, it remained an option, and an attractive one at that. The primary obstacle to being released from this whole humiliating mess sat at the breakfast table with him, completely unaware of the storm going on outside.

Ada, at least, knew something was wrong. She laughed a little bell-peal of laughter and touched Eric's face. She didn't notice how he flinched at her touch when she said, "Look, Uncle Eric! You look like someone painted your face white!"

"I suppose I do, darling." He kissed the top of her head. "It's simply work problems, nothing you need to worry your magical little self about."

Between Eric, Dan, and Hadiya, they got Ada fed and changed quickly enough. It was a good thing they did because they ended up having guests sooner than they expected. Agents Gomes and Rourke showed up by about nine thirty, parking their giant gas-guzzling, government-issue SUV right in front of the house in a no-parking area. It wouldn't get ticketed. Anyone could see it was a law enforcement vehicle.

With any luck, it would keep journalists farther back than normal.

Dan showed them into the library. "I have to assume you gentlemen aren't here to arrest Eric for anything."

193

Gomes, who stood a little above six feet and was the kind of stunningly beautiful man that made people's heads turn, gave Dan a funny look. "Has he done something we should be arresting him for? I'm pretty sure we'd be on shaky ground, arresting a foreign royal, but I'm always better about asking for forgiveness than permission."

Rourke, who might have been fifteen years older than Gomes and had a funny little D'Artagnan goatee, nudged his partner. "Don't tease them, Gomes. It's rude." He shook his head, a rueful grin on his face. "Apologies. He's got a funny sense of humor. It's what comes of mostly chasing serial killers as a career. We'd planned to stop by to update you about your siblings' case, but we found out about the, er, home movie and did a little bit of digging."

Dan put his hand on Eric's back, giving him support and strength. "You have to know he had nothing to do with that film. It was filmed without his knowledge or consent."

Gomes' face lost its humor. "Yeah, our video guys picked up on that." He tugged at his collar. "We should probably all sit down." He took his own advice, folding himself into a seat on the couch. "Listen. We have a whole separate team in Virginia dedicated to child pornography. Rourke and I might show up to make a bust, but we don't

194

do the research and we don't handle the evidence. We did the math, realized what was going on, and made a call or two."

Rourke snorted. "They're your contacts, Luis. It's okay to admit it."

Gomes glared. "It's not about credit, Kev. I mean yeah, there's a certain amount of crossover, but they don't care about that. Anyway, some of my contacts back at Quantico were able to do a little bit of analysis. While the video was filmed years ago, it was uploaded from a location right here in Boston. We're tracking down the culprit."

"It was my brother." Eric took a deep breath. "It was my brother, or someone working for him." He moistened his lips and kept his eyes on a book across the room. "And the scene was filmed in Corvia. Since it was Andreas filming it, it wasn't considered to be illegal there."

"You're shitting me." Dan stared at him. "You researched this already."

Rourke smirked. "It wasn't illegal there, but uploading child pornography is very illegal here and it doesn't matter who's doing it. Which you already know, since we've been advised you already took legal action against any outlets sharing the film or using images from it."

Dan grinned, still staring at Eric. "Nice."

Eric shook his head. "I'm not looking to make money. It goes to an organization to support human trafficking victims. I'm very fortunate to be in the position I am, and what was done was relatively mild—"

Dan covered his hand with his own. "The hell it was. Your brother deliberately recorded you in an intimate moment, used it against you with your father, and then both of your siblings used the recording to try to blackmail you into things you wouldn't be willing to do otherwise. You had to leave home, you couldn't go back to your mother's country, and you had to actually seek asylum in the US. Even though you're a damn prince."

Eric fought against the bile rising in his throat. "Yes, it's true. But I had the wherewithal to support myself. There are others who are forced into worse situations who cannot escape. I can help them, I should help them, and I do help them. Quietly. This is just one more way for me to do so."

"That's admirable." Gomes nodded slowly. "But if we can find the person who did this, then the crime is actionable."

Eric didn't need to be told that. He let out a sigh. "If you don't think it will jeopardize the case against my sister's killer, I certainly won't stop you. I don't think it's likely to be worth your time—a jury won't convict someone for humiliating a gay foreigner. But I'm not going to stop you."

Agent Gomes winked at him. "Once upon a time, you'd have been right. But us gay foreigners have to look out for each other, right? If nothing else, he'll have to defend against the charges, and that's going to be embarrassing for a prince.

"We did initially come to update you on your sister's case. We got a lead on the technology used to drive the autonomous car into your sister's vehicle. Now *that* took some wrangling, and finding a way to get the information that we can use in court was fun, but apparently, it's experimental technology that's only in the hands of the Corvian Secret Service."

Eric didn't have trouble staying calm for that one. "It fits. The only person with a motive is Andreas."

"We agree." Rourke bit the inside of his cheek. "I'm not sure we can prove much beyond that at this point. We won't be able to get a warrant to search his property, and we couldn't arrest him anyway."

"I know." Eric bowed his head. "He's willing to do anything to get to Ada."

Dan stood up. "Don't you think it's a little bit weird that he's so gung-ho to get to Ada? I mean, he tried to kidnap Ada once before, apparently."

"The most that can be done is expelling him from the country. And that's going to take some doing. Our best bet is proving the kiddie porn." Gomes jerked his head toward Eric.

Eric had known, or suspected, as much.

The doorbell rang, again.

Dan glanced at the agents, who stiffened. "I don't suppose that's friends of yours."

The agents shook their heads. "Want us to chase them off?"

Dan headed toward the door. "Nah. I'll get it. With any luck, it's someone else with something useful to add."

Eric watched him go. He couldn't help but wish Dan had stayed—but he didn't get to have people stay.

The reason why walked back into the library behind Dan. It had been more than ten years, but Eric would recognize Lian Meindl anywhere.

Of course, Lian had aged well. He'd had those bones, the kind of structure that would hold up no matter what time did to him. Eric had thought him beautiful at twenty-two, but now, in his midthirties, he'd clearly hit his prime. His chest was a wall of muscle, even inside that tailored suit he wore. His hair was soft and blond, without a

198

trace of gray, and his blue eyes full of as much mirth as they'd been when he and Eric had met.

"Well, isn't this a lovely reunion?" Lian spoke in German, even though no one else in the room came from Corvia. "You've grown up, Eric."

"Most people do grow, between fifteen and twenty-eight." Eric had to draw on every bit of his reserves to keep himself steady. He spoke in English because he hadn't been raised in a barn, and he knew damn well Lian was fluent. "Lian Meindl, meet my personal security chief, Daniel Marshall, and Agents Gomes and Rourke from the FBI. Lian, I had no idea you were in the United States."

He didn't invite Lian to sit. He didn't want Lian staining his home—Ada's home, it wasn't going to be Eric's for much longer—the way he'd stained Eric himself. It was probably the wrong way to think about it—in a very real way, Lian had been a victim too. Still, after everything, Eric couldn't change the way he felt.

"Ah. Well, I wasn't, but my boss called and asked me to swing by with something of his. Something important." He smirked, eyes still dancing with laughter. "I'm sure you've already figured out what it was, a smart boy like you."

Eric met Agent Gomes' eyes. Had he truly believed himself in love with someone this stupid?

199

He knew it wasn't love *now*, but at fifteen he'd been simply besotted.

"Ah, yes. The video." Eric rolled his eyes. "I suppose you gave it to him to upload?"

Lian spotted the bar and fixed himself a drink. It wasn't even eleven yet, but here he was day-drinking. "Are you insane? His Highness would never. I'm not sure he knows how, since we're being honest. That's what he keeps me around for. I've been his technical support manager for fifteen years."

Eric stared at him.

Lian flopped down into one of the empty chairs and took a deep gulp from his glass. "You look surprised. You have to have known—then again, they did give you the bum's rush out of the country after everything. Even His Highness didn't expect quite such a good result. Yes, I was working for the crown prince well before we met. He hired me, Eric. He hired me to go and be your little boyfriend.

"I'm not actually gay. I have a wife. I have three beautiful children, who I love dearly. I'll have to bring them something back from Harvard, don't you think? I usually do, when I travel for His Highness."

Eric held himself immobile. It was the only way to avoid falling to pieces. He could feel the eyes of everyone in the room on him, just waiting to see him buckle. It wasn't that much different from last time. "Fascinating. I suppose that will be a proud tale for the grandchildren someday."

Agent Gomes caught his eye. Right—Eric was supposed to be doing something.

"So—you're the one who uploaded the video, even though it showed you having sex with a minor?"

Lian scoffed and took another deep drink. "There is no age of consent in Corvia."

"There is, actually, and it's eighteen. But you uploaded it when? I'm just curious—I know it hit at five local time—"

Lian laughed, loud and shrill. "I didn't even know what he wanted to do with it until I landed."

It was all the confession Gomes and Rourke needed. Gomes hauled Lian to his feet while Rourke cuffed him and read him his rights.

"You can't arrest me!" Lian's shouts drowned out Rourke's recitation. "I'm with the prince's delegation! I'm immune!"

"I'm looking forward to testing that in court." Gomes grinned, savage and insincere. "In the meantime, we're taking a trip to Chelsea. And then, you're going to take a little trip down to Nashua Street and to general population. Be sure to tell everyone all about your royal connections, sugarplum."

Chapter Eighteen

Dan had to hand it to Eric. He didn't show a single sign of being disturbed by anything that had happened that day while Ada was awake. He even let her meet the FBI agents who'd arrested his former boyfriend, if that was what anyone could call this Lian guy. He had plenty of phone calls to make and things to do, but he went through them all with his usual preternatural calm.

If anything, it was Dan who was freaking out. He did his best to hold things together, but he had to update Levi on the situation and couldn't hold everything back. "Christ on a cracker, Levi, I didn't think things could get worse, but they did. It turns out that video was made on purpose. The brother actually paid one of his employees to go out and seduce Eric, just so he could humiliate him and tear him down in front of their father."

Levi sighed. "You know, I wish I could say I was surprised, but nothing with this family surprises me anymore. I thought my family was screwed up, but these folks take the cake. I got the message from those feds. I don't think we'd be able to prove murder, not enough to expel Andreas from the country. But there's nothing that's going to convince me he didn't do it."

"Same." Dan's stomach lurched, and he barely made it to the trash barrel before he lost his breakfast. "Sorry."

"Dan, you've survived worse without blinking an eye. I'm not judging, I just want to know. What's got you so tied up in knots you're puking in the corner back there in Boston?"

Dan wiped his mouth. Levi was too smart for his own good. "I don't know. I might be too close to this. It's Ada, it's Ben, it's Eric—"

Levi chuckled softly. "Yeah. I suspected as much. It seemed like you were more attached than I'd have expected."

"I know, it's unprofessional, I'm sorry." Dan slumped to the floor and huddled in on himself.

"Under the circumstances? I'd be surprised if there wasn't some attraction. He's easy on the eyes, you're in forced proximity, and you've got a shared area of concern in the little girl. He also seems to be a pretty decent guy. I'm not mad. I do think you need to figure out what you want to do going forward. It's not my place as your boss to tell you one way or the other, but if you want to stick around in Boston, there are ways of making that happen."

Dan rubbed his face. "He says he's giving me the house and custody of Ada once it's all over."

Levi hesitated. "That doesn't sound good. I thought you guys have a thing."

"Yeah. I mean, I don't know. Something's going on, but I don't know how long it would last for. I like *him*. His family sucks. And I know exactly what I'm talking about." Dan let out a semihysterical laugh. "Mine's not exactly a prize; I mean, he filed a lawsuit to keep my dad away from Ada until he sobers up, but I'd take my dad and his friendship with Mr. Walker over that bunch of poisoned apples any day of the week."

"You've got that right. I spoke with a reporter from Corvia. Apparently, the royal guards have had to intervene between Andreas and his wife and kid a few times. They get together for appearance's sake, in public, but they're living in separate wings of the palace and the guards won't let him near them."

Dan groaned. "Which explains why Andreas is so desperate to get Ada back. The younger half siblings aren't producing and aren't likely to turn out heirs anyone would want, and

Ada would be a good way to appease a public getting increasingly tired of royal antics."

"So having one of his top aides arrested puts Eric in even more danger." Levi dropped his voice. "Andreas is someone who is used to getting his own way. He's already been thwarted twice—when the guards intervened to keep him away from his wife and kid, and when Eric inherited Ada. Then Eric went and had Andreas' top aide arrested. How do you think that would go over with any other abuser?"

Dan cringed. "We might need you to send in the cavalry."

"I'll see who's available. The feds are involved, which makes things challenging. So does Andreas' status as a foreign official." Levi cleared his throat. "You're really going to have to step up here, Dan, but I know you can do it."

Dan sucked in his cheeks for a second. "Yeah. You're right. I can. It's my job, and I want to do it. I want to protect him. I just—"

"You just wish you could separate the man from the family? Yeah, I hear that." Levi laughed a little. "From what it sounds like though, that's mostly been done already. It's just a matter of keeping him safe from them too."

Dan managed to sit up straight. "Thanks, Levi. That's the right way to look at it." He finished the call, cleaned up his mess, and got back to work locking down the property.

The property did need to be locked down, even though more than half of the work had already been done. Tourists covered the sidewalk outside. Any one of them could be an assassin, sent by Andreas to get Eric out of the way once and for all. For that matter, Eric's legal maneuverings would have angered people involved with the child pornography industry, and those folks were just as dangerous as Andreas. In a lot of ways, they were worse.

Dan caught a reporter going through their mail, another one going through their trash bins (which were behind the house, not on the curb, so not public property), and still another trying to climb the gutter to get a glimpse through an upstairs window. In each instance, the tourists helped by raising a hue and cry, letting Dan know there was something to see. Eric ordered water and snacks to be delivered to the tourists as a thank-you.

Cambridge police stepped in then, both because they couldn't just have people trespassing on other people's property and because the tourists were becoming a hazard. Eric still didn't say anything until after Ada was put to bed.

Only then did Eric sink onto a sofa in the library, martini in hand. "I've treasured every minute of privacy I've had since I was fifteen years old." He glanced over at Dan and then back at his drink. "The house is more house than I've ever needed, but I bought it because it was enough to guarantee my privacy. After this is over, it should be enough to keep you and Ada safe and private—but I can't promise anything. Now that the location is out there, you might want to sell it and take Ada someplace else, someplace easier to secure."

Dan counted to five. Then he sat beside Eric. "I know your plan has been to give me custody of Ada and the house. Are you doing that because you legitimately don't want them or because you think you should?"

Eric blinked at him. "I love Ada. It's the best solution for her. She loves you, she needs to not be exposed to this circus, and she deserves much better than anything I can give her."

Dan considered his options. He'd never been a *words* kind of guy. He did action, and he was proud of it. This wasn't a problem he could punch, shoot, or detonate. He had to use delicacy and tact. "Well, I appreciate that you think I'm a good option for her. I'd do anything for her, and she does know me.

"But, Eric, you've shown you're actually a pretty good dad. Guardian. Whatever. You're incredible with Ada, and you've taken to parenting like a fish takes to water. I know you never spent time with young children in your life, but here you are holding hands, choosing food, and playing dumb board games like you've been doing it your whole life. I know you're all academic and you're a genius and all that, but you are *good* at this too.

"Ada loves you. She loves spending time with you. And I know we haven't known each other long, but I'm enjoying spending time with you too."

Eric choked on his martini. "Dan, think about what you're saying. I'm disgusting. I let myself get seduced by one of my brother's aides. The entire world has seen me losing my virginity—"

The growl that escaped from Dan's throat surprised even Dan. "That son of a bitch should be grateful he's in jail right now because no place in the world would be safe for him. I didn't know he was your first."

Eric rolled his eyes. "It's hardly his fault. He was paid to do a job, and he did it."

"It's absolutely his fault. It's not like anyone was going to die if he said no. It's not like it was a life-or-death situation. You were a child. He preyed on your inexperience to take what should have been a joyful moment and turn it into a weapon against you, and he knew exactly what he was doing at the time. And then he had the gall to come here and try to lord it over you, all these years later.

"Eric, listen to me." Dan took Eric's free hand. "None of that was your fault. You're an amazing man. You don't need to be penalized for the rest of your life because someone did something to hurt you, okay?"

Eric didn't withdraw his hand, but he didn't squeeze back either. It sat there, limp. "I have to take responsibility for my own behavior, Dan. I appreciate your attempt to build me up a bit—"

Dan laughed. He couldn't help it. "I'm not the build-someone-up type. I legitimately believe this. And so do you—when it applies to someone else."

Eric stiffened. "It's different. I knew I could be targeted, or at least I should have known—"

"You were a child. And you didn't grow up with your family, around all the royal bullshit. You were acting like any other fifteen-year-old would. You should have had someone else looking out for you, but it's in the past. Look—you're not going to change your mindset around this because some guy said something to you once.

210

"I need you to know that I want you around. Not for your money, not for your title. I want you around because you're smart, because you're interesting, and because you're one of the strongest people I know. And that's saying something, considering that I was a Ranger. Okay?"

Eric pulled his hand back. "You can't let someone like me around Ada long-term. She'll find out about that tape someday."

"And she'll learn that life goes on even when shitty people do shitty things. She'll learn they can be resilient, just like their Uncle Eric. And she'll learn not to judge people at school when something similar happens because there's more to the story. Damn it, Eric, I love you, and I'm not going to stop until you love you too."

Eric stared at him. "You've completely lost your mind."

Dan laughed again. "Maybe. It doesn't change anything. I'm not leaving you, Eric. We're in this together."

Chapter Nineteen

Eric spent the night in his own room. He didn't want to. Everything in him told him to crawl into Dan's bed, to take him up on the sweet offer he'd made and accept the comfort and safety he wanted to give.

Hadn't that been what got Eric into this mess in the first place?

He didn't think he'd ever been in love with Lian, not for real. He also didn't dare let himself fall in love. Even puppy love had come close to killing him once. To find out Dan was playing a part, after Eric had let him in this far, would be like a nuclear bomb to his psyche. He needed to keep his head in the game right now.

Apparently, Lian lacked the stamina for life in an American prison. After one night in the general population at the Nashua Street jail, he was willing to do whatever he had to in order to get out. He freely admitted to having uploaded the video of

213

himself and Eric, at Andreas' behest. He said Andreas must have known it was illegal, since he was a dignitary who'd sat in on multiple discussions about child pornography at the international level.

It didn't get him very far. The judge declined bail, determining him to be a flight risk. His passport was not a diplomatic one, so the embassy could be of no help to him even if they wanted to. And they did not seem to want to, given the seriousness of the charge. They did help to provide him an attorney.

Eric got a call from Lian's wife at noon. Her name was Maria. She wept, sobbed, and screamed at him. He didn't let it bother him, at least not much. She apparently hadn't known about her husband's activity prior to his marriage and insisted he was "only doing his duty."

"This is your revenge on him, then? Condemning him to rot in prison because he loved me instead of you?"

Eric sighed and passed a hand over his face. She couldn't see him, of course, and it was just as well. "Maria, I'm very sorry you're going through this. I understand you have three children? I believe he said that yesterday. It's a lot for you to have to endure, and so suddenly. I can't imagine what

214

you're feeling, what people are saying to you or your sons.

"Your husband isn't in jail for what he did to me in Corvia all those years ago. I would never have looked for revenge, or even to reconnect with him. All I've wanted was to put it behind me. Please understand this. After—well, after *that*—I was forced to flee not one but two countries. I had no home, no friends, nothing. I've lived under my mother's name just so I'd never have to think about the past again.

"Your husband is in jail because he did something that is illegal in the United States, while he was in the United States. He knew it was illegal, and he bragged about doing it in front of two people he knew were law enforcement officers. I didn't press charges. I couldn't have encouraged or stopped these charges from being filed. He put his foot right in the shit and then he ground it in." The coarse turn of phrase felt alien on his tongue, more appropriate to Dan than to him.

"You're lying." She sniffed, voice much more moderate now. "It has to be something you did. Everyone knows about you."

Yes, everyone knew about Eric. One more reason to turn away from everything Dan had to give. "Yes, I suppose everyone does. Believe whatever helps you to get through this, Maria. The

215

truth is, Lian seduced a teenager and allowed himself to be filmed doing so in order to satisfy a jealous older sibling. Over ten years later, Lian posted a copy of that film to the internet. What *everyone* knows about me doesn't matter much in the greater scheme of things. These are the facts. It doesn't matter that he did what he thought was his duty by Prince Andreas. The fact is Andreas will let him rot in jail now that he's no longer useful.

"If the Crown doesn't help to cover your expenses, don't hesitate to get in touch. Neither you nor your children should suffer for what Lian and Andreas did. I hope you find peace."

And with that, Eric hung up. Maria might be hurting, and she might be angry. Eric didn't need to make himself available to be her target.

Dan appeared after a little while, once Ada had gone down for her nap. "I don't know if this is helpful or not, but Andreas was on that crappy fake news channel talking about this whole mess. He didn't manage to come off well, but then again I'm biased as hell."

Eric huffed out a little laugh, but he stiffened as Dan came up behind him and rubbed at his shoulders. "Dan, this doesn't—"

"I love you, Eric. And I think you love me, even if you aren't ready to address it. I can't blame you." Dan bent down and kissed the top of Eric's

216

head. "Honestly, I can't imagine how I'd handle any of that. But I'm not going to stand by and force you to go through all this shit by yourself."

Eric's hand trembled, and for once, he didn't try to hide it. He let it show instead. The whole world knew how weak he was. What did it matter now? "I don't have anything to offer you."

Dan scoffed. "I'm not looking for anything. Just you. You're enough for me." He kissed Eric's cheek. "We've got a real shot, I think, at building something strong here. You, me, Ada. We can make this work—but that's not why I came in here. The last thing I want to do is pressure you."

Eric managed to smile. "I wish you understood the way in which your very existence is pressure, and relieves pressure at the same time. You're a paradox, and I don't do well with paradoxes." He turned to face Dan again, but his phone interrupted them.

The incoming call was from King Sebastian. Of course Eric's father would choose now to reach out.

Eric sighed and put the call on speaker. "Good afternoon, Your Majesty."

Sebastian harrumphed. "You're speaking English. Why are you speaking English? Is that shaved ape with you? He is, isn't he? You've put me on speaker. I demand you take me off speaker

217

at once. This is a family call, and whatever you may be doing with that pervert, he is not family."

Eric raised an eyebrow at Dan, who shrugged.

"Apologies, Your Majesty, but Dan Marshall is my head of security. At this point, having conversations with anyone connected to Andreas separate from Mr. Marshall seems like an exceedingly ill-advised idea. And we do share guardianship of Ada, which makes him family in any event."

"That holds no force in Corvian law." Sebastian's accent, when he spoke English, was harsh. He had no trouble finding words though. He used English in diplomacy all the time. Eric had no worries about his ability to conduct a conversation. "Send him away."

"Absolutely not. If Your Majesty wishes to speak with me, you'll have to do so in front of Mr. Marshall. Can I assume you're calling on Andreas' behalf?" Part of Eric quaked at the thought of standing up to his father in this way, but he wasn't going to be deterred. Not now.

"What's all this nonsense about you having his top aide arrested? Simply drop the charges and have the man released. It's childish, Eric, and not becoming of a prince."

218

Eric laughed, but there wasn't any humor in it. "I haven't been a prince since you and my mother divorced. Not really. And even if somehow I counted as royal, this is America. There is no royalty here. I didn't 'have him arrested.' He confessed to a crime in front of law enforcement. They had no choice but to arrest him. I had nothing to do with it. My understanding is the man has a wife and three young children. Can I assume they'll be taken care of while this works its way through the American legal system?"

"What? They aren't my problem." Sebastian sounded flabbergasted.

"On the contrary, under Corvian law I believe they are. Lian was acting under Andreas' direct orders when he committed the crime on American soil. I don't care if their pay comes out of the crown prince's budget or simply out of the Crown's, but they should be cared for just as much as anyone else harmed in the occasion of royal business."

Sebastian growled for a moment, but he didn't push back any further. "Why do you care what happens to them? Isn't this Lian fellow the one you disgraced yourself with? I'd think you'd be happy to think of the woman he replaced you with suffering."

219

Eric rolled his eyes to the ceiling. "That's because you don't know me well at all, Your Majesty. Lian was paid to seduce me, by Andreas, for the sole purpose of further alienating me from you. And it worked, I must say, given that we haven't spoken since Andreas first showed you that video."

"Don't make up stories to try to make yourself look innocent."

"I heard Lian admit it himself." Dan spoke up now. "So did two federal agents. I'm sure they'd be happy to discuss it with you. You can believe what you want, but it's the truth."

"You're not part of this discussion. You're just a mercenary. Andreas told me all about you."

"This would be the same son who paid a man to seduce your teenage son and filmed it, right? The same one who's going to be publicly arrested for child pornography?" Dan laughed, low and cruel. "I'm not so sure I'd be putting his point of view at the top of the heap, but you do you."

"You disgust me. You can't think I'll let two homosexuals raise my grandchild, do you? Your filth and perversion must be stopped."

"I'm pretty sure you set a new standard for filth and perversion with your own antics back in the seventies." Dan shrugged. "Selene told me all about you. She was pretty sure that her child

220

shouldn't ever be allowed near her Corvian family. That's why she left her to Eric here. You made that happen, by the way. You created the environment that led to all of that. I mean, yeah, Andreas did the crimes, but you made it acceptable—"

"They cannot arrest a foreign prince!"

"They can't *try* a foreign prince." Eric cut through his father's shouting. "They can't incarcerate a foreign prince. They can arrest him— and they can do so publicly. They can expel him from the country and ensure he isn't welcome back."

"They should do it to you. I can't believe they let a slut like you into the country in the first place, one who lies about his brother and —"

Dan hung up the phone. "I think that's about enough of that."

Eric gaped at him. "You just hung up on the king of Corvia!"

"I'm probably the first person to do that—well, ever, actually. Come on. We've got a lot of planning to do. We've got a little girl to protect.

If you think Andreas is going to be stopped just because we stood up to his dad, you're not nearly as smart as people've given you credit for."

Eric stood and kissed Dan. "You're right. And Dan?"

"Hm?"

"Thank you."

Chapter Twenty

Dan didn't sleep well that night. It wasn't so much the anxiety as the noise. Andreas was still putting himself and his version of events in the news, while Eric's attorneys and anyone with common sense were countering with the obvious "child porn is bad" narrative. This kept the house in the public eye, with plenty of people wanting to get a sense of who this person at the center of all this controversy might be.

It wasn't like Dan wasn't used to getting his sleep in limited doses. He'd doze for a couple of hours, get up, and take a twirl around the perimeter just to check on everything. The fact that it was Boston instead of any of a dozen war zones he'd survived might have made it clearer, but it didn't make much more of a difference than that.

Eric wasn't sleeping much either. He prowled around the house like a grumpy cat, occasionally disappearing into his office or his bedroom. Dan tried to soothe him as best he could, but there was only so much he could do. Nothing was going to get better until Andreas was out of the country, and it was possible it wouldn't get better even then. Everything depended on how well they managed to neutralize Andreas.

The next day brought them a visitor, who showed up not long after they'd finished cleaning up after breakfast. Eric bristled when Dan let Ted into the house, but he didn't say anything. Dan had to be grateful. He knew Eric wasn't thrilled, but when Ada saw "Grampy" and ran to give him a giant hug, he didn't make a scene.

Mary Ann had come along too, and she asked Ada to show her her bedroom. "I'd love to see where you're sleeping, darling." She simpered at Ada and offered her hand, although not without darting a vicious glower in Eric's direction.

Dan knew what this was about. It was an attempt to get Dan and Eric alone. At least Dan hoped that was all it was. He didn't think his mother would try to spirit Ada away, but then again anything was possible. He caught Hadiya's eye, and she nodded, following quietly and without attracting Mary Ann's attention.

At least that was one less thing to be worried about.

Eric led Ted into the library. "Can I offer you some coffee?" There was no warmth in his tone, and from the look on Ted's face, Ted didn't expect there to be any.

"No. I wouldn't take anything from this house anyway. You need to send that kid home with us, and you need to do it today. I don't give a crap about lawyers or laws or any of that nonsense. You made a porno, and now it's all over the place. Half the planet's seen you doing things no man should do." Ted shook his finger in Eric's face.

Dan didn't think. He slid himself between his father and his partner. "Dad, back the fuck off."

His father's eyes bulged, but what really hit Dan was the sudden sharp intake of breath from Eric.

Ted missed it, or he didn't care. "I am your father. You don't get to speak to me that way. Ben would have shown some respect."

That one hurt, but Dan wasn't about to let his father lash out at Eric like that. "Ben wouldn't have been in a position where he had to get between you and Selene. You have no right to come into his home and start—"

"I wouldn't have had to come and try to get the kid away from Selene because Selene was a good girl. She wasn't a perverted whore!" Ted lunged for Eric.

Dan grabbed his father's shoulders and pushed him, gently but firmly, into a seat. "One more time and I will remove you from this house. Eric has custody. Not you. Not Andreas. You don't know what's going on with that video."

"I know it exists. It's bad enough that he does those things with men, but to make a movie of it—" Ted turned his head and spat onto the rug.

"The 'movie' was made without his knowledge or consent. He was a child. He was a victim." Anger made Dan shake. If this were anyone but his father, they'd be a bloody mess on the ground by now.

"Oh, sure, that's what he says now. And you're dumb enough to believe him. If he hadn't put himself in that position, there wouldn't be a tape. There's no victims—"

Dan hauled his father to his feet. "All right. That's enough. You've outlasted your welcome."

He dragged Ted to the door, just in time to hear Ada screaming from upstairs.

"I've got it," Eric said, racing toward the staircase.

Dan didn't like where this was going, but he kept right on pushing his father out the front door.

Ted didn't manage to get out of his grip until he was on the brick walkway leading up to the front door. "You mark my words. He's going to turn Ada into a whore too."

"If you call my boyfriend a whore one more time, I'm going to forget you put a roof over my head for eighteen years. You were grudging enough about it." Dan crossed his arms over his chest. "Don't ever let me catch you or Ma darkening his doorstep again, am I clear? It's going to take a court order to even get supervised visitation, and I'm fighting that every step of the way. You're a poison, old man, and I'm going to make sure you don't infect my girl."

The crowd cheered. Ted turned to stare. These weren't hostile crowds. A few people had Corvian flags. A few others had homemade signs or cloth banners with messages of support. Others had rainbow flags and banners. *We love Prince Eric! We Stand With Our Prince! Long Live the Professor Prince! Believe Victims!*

Ted cringed and slunk away as the crowd jeered. Dan retreated back into the house, trying to make it look strong and purposeful instead of like he was staggering.

Shouting from the upstairs, as well as Ada's shrieks, reminded him of his duty. He locked the door and reset the alarm before racing up to join Eric in Ada's bedroom.

There, Hadiya had put herself between Ada and Mary Ann. Mary Ann held her hand out to Ada while waving a pink backpack in the other. Eric stood just inside the doorway with his phone in his hand.

Ada's face was almost as red as her hair, and her arm had the marks of an adult's fingers on it. "I'm not going anywhere with you, Grammy! I wanna live with Uncle Dan and Uncle Eric! I love them! You're mean!"

"They're not right for you. You're just a child, you don't know what's right. I'm your grandma."

"You will not take her." Hadiya didn't raise her voice, but she didn't have to. Somehow, the low growl she let out was scarier than the loudest shout. "I will do anything I have to do to keep her, or anyone else Prince Eric cares about, safe."

"You're just some tarted-up girl—"

Eric handed the phone off to Dan and stepped forward. "Excuse me. Thank you, Dan. Your husband has been removed from the premises. Hadiya, would you be so kind as to call the authorities? Mrs. Marshall has attempted a noncustodial abduction and has harmed my niece."

He slipped his arm under Mary Ann's. From the outside, it looked almost like a warm embrace as he ushered Mary Ann quickly from Ada's bedroom.

Dan knew his mother could no more resist than she could fight the tide. He slipped out to follow as Eric took Mary Ann to the door.

His mother sputtered the whole time. "You have no right to keep her from me. I am her grandmother! You're just an unnatural—"

"You bruised my niece. You can hate me as much as you want. I don't care. I've been willing to overlook the favoritism you've shown toward your other son because of your grief. I have one purpose, and that is to guard my niece over everything else. I was willing to put my distaste toward you aside and give you some contact, but you've proved that was the wrong decision." He pushed her out the door.

It was the first time he saw the nature of the crowd outside, and the first time they saw Eric. They roared with delight as Mary Ann stumbled out the door into the waiting arms of Cambridge police officers. Dan passed the phone back to Eric and leaned over as the older-looking officer asked if Eric wanted to press charges.

"I think I have to." Eric sighed. "I'll post their bail too, so long as they stay away from us. I don't hate them, but I do need to go through the proper process to ensure they can't do this again."

"Fair enough." Dan felt a pang as his mother was cuffed, but it was only a small one. She'd tried to kidnap a child and bruised her too. "We'll send a detective over to get pictures and a statement from the little girl."

"Thank you very much." Eric glanced back at the crowd, who cheered again as Mary Ann was led away. "Er. Is this . . ."

"Your public." Dan huffed out a little laugh. The crowd was a nightmare, from a security perspective. From a public relations standpoint, they were an absolute necessity. "You should wave or something. Let them feel validated."

"The whole point of living here is not being *Prince Eric*." Eric hissed the words, so only Dan could hear him, and waved and smiled for the crowd.

The people ate it up. What was it about so much of humanity, even in America, that made them so excited about the presence of a certain combination of genes? Eric was a prince, but he was so much more than an accident of birth and privilege.

A murmur rose up from the back of the crowd. The hairs on the back of Dan's neck rose. Nothing good ever came from a shift like that. A few heads over near the back of the crowd jerked away from something near the center, like they'd been pushed, and finally, Dan saw a familiar artfully-tousled mop of blond hair moving through the throng. A pair of anonymous heads from the Diplomatic Security Service joined him. If Dan had to guess, he'd assume they were the source of the shoving.

"Get back in the house." He turned to Eric. "Now."

Eric didn't push back. He just waved to the crowd again, a royal smile still plastered on his face, and stepped back through the door. Dan followed him.

Andreas and his diplomatic service goons were too fast. The first goon got a foot in the door and held it open for Andreas, while the other followed him through.

Eric glanced at Dan, just for a moment. "Dan, would you be so kind as to ask Hadiya to put Ada down for her nap?" His voice made it sound like he was just asking about the weather, and his limbs didn't tremble at all. Only the tiny spots of color in his cheeks hinted at the fear in his heart.

Dan didn't fight him. He hated the idea of leaving Eric alone with Andreas or letting him have any contact with such a sleazy excuse for a sibling. Ada was the priority though. Eric had been clear about that from the beginning.

He raced up the stairs to find Hadiya already ushering Ada toward the hiding place. Ada's face had gone from red to pasty white, so it was clear to Dan that she knew her uncle was on the property. He shepherded them to the ancient hiding place. They knew to stay silent and hidden.

Then Dan called the two FBI agents who'd been working on Ben's case. Gomes picked up right away. Somehow, Dan wasn't surprised.

"Mr. Marshall. What's going on?"

"Agent Gomes. Thank God. My parents just tried to abduct Ada, and now, Andreas just forced his way into the house."

"Well, fuck. We're on our way. I'll send Cambridge PD—they'll be there before we can get there." Gomes hung up.

Dan was already on his way back downstairs, Glock in hand. He could hear Andreas shouting, but he was choosing to shout in German. Apparently, this was another of those "family discussions."

Eric's response was in English, and again spoken with perfect sangfroid. "Andreas, I know you're not this stupid. I'm not sending Ada with you, and no, I don't care that you have a gun. Do you even know how to use that thing? You've never dirtied your hands a day in your life."

The sound of the gun firing was the loudest thing Dan had ever heard.

Chapter Twenty-One

The gears in Eric's mind turned in overtime as he raced through the different possibilities. Andreas was standing in front of him. He'd forced his way into the house, and he had a gun. Somehow, Eric didn't think Andreas had showed up to discuss mutual defense from paparazzi.

Andreas was ranting at him in German, which meant he didn't want anyone else to be able to hold his words against him. The men from Diplomatic Security stood silent and useless, although their pallor made it clear that they were concerned about the situation. It would have been fabulous if they decided to help, but Eric supposed they weren't here to enforce laws or protect Americans.

Not that Eric was American, in any way that counted.

Andreas was still shouting. Blah, blah, obedience, blah, blah, duty, blah blah. Eric had

235

heard it all before, although not quite at such volume. None of it mattered, so Eric tuned it out the way he'd tuned out every bully he'd ever met. He needed to focus.

Eric had missed out on any kind of military service. He'd been too young for compulsory national service when either of his countries wanted him, and then he'd been banished. Many people took that lack, as well as his physique and his sexuality, to mean he was weak. And Eric *was* weak, compared to warriors like Dan.

Dan, who had to keep Ada safe.

More than one of the schools at which Eric had been housed through his youth had insisted on "training" as part of their educational regimen, and while Eric had been given no reprieve because of his youth or small size, he'd learned to turn both into advantages. He remembered one lesson from a grizzled instructor at one school in Iran, one his mother had dumped him in early in his career.

Dr. Shirvani taught poetry, but he also taught "readiness." The boys all thought he was a joke because he'd lost a leg and an arm in the war, but he could kick all of their asses from the school to the border and back again. *It's always to your advantage when the enemy underestimates you,* he'd told Eric with a wink.

Eric had never forgotten.

236

And so he huffed and rolled his eyes. He spoke in English because he wanted someone to be able to testify later if this all went south. The guys from Diplomatic Security would probably continue to be useless, but Dan could almost certainly still hear him.

"Andreas, I know you're not this stupid. I'm not sending Ada with you, and no, I don't care that you have a gun. Do you even know how to use that thing? You've never dirtied your hands a day in your life."

It was a goad, a taunt calculated to drive Andreas to action. While Eric hadn't been able to serve either of his countries because of his sexuality, Andreas had opted not to serve because of his position as crown prince. He was sensitive about the appearance of laziness, so it was the perfect goad.

Andreas turned scarlet and raised the gun.

This was the riskiest part. Eric stepped in and grabbed Andreas' wrist, jerking his gun hand down and toward him. At the same time, he brought his elbow down with every bit of force he could muster against Andreas' elbow.

Andreas fired at the same time.

Everything Eric had read claimed people didn't feel the pain of a gunshot wound at first. Those authors had clearly lied. The bullet felt like pure fire, molten metal pouring straight into Eric's calf. He ground his teeth as his knee buckled, transferring weight to his remaining good leg, and redirected his elbow into Andreas' chin.

It was an awkward hit, but Andreas had just had his elbow dislocated. It was enough. He dropped the damn gun.

One of the useless Diplomatic Security agents jumped in to secure the gun, just as Dan raced down the stairs with his own gun drawn. "What the fuck?"

The other guard stepped between Andreas and Eric, which could only be a good thing because Eric couldn't hold himself up anymore. He fell to the ground as his trousers cooled around his lower leg. *Blood*, he identified, as though it were happening to someone else.

Someone slammed on the door, hard and authoritative. "Cambridge Police! Open up!"

Dan glanced at the men from Diplomatic Security. "I swear to God if that ass isn't restrained by the time I get back—" He left his threat unsaid and went to let the police in.

Eric tried to breathe through the pain. It was over, or at least it soon would be. He'd go to a hospital, Andreas would be expelled from the country—at least, he hoped Andreas would be

238

expelled. Attempted fratricide would have to be enough to get the job done, right?

Uniformed officers, with their guns drawn, flooded Eric's home and surrounded Andreas. This got the officers from Diplomatic Security riled, but they knew they were on shaky ground. They conferred between themselves and called their supervisor, on the grounds that "We don't get paid enough for this shit."

Eric lay in a heap on the floor, until the police finally let Dan come to him. "We're going to need an ambulance here," Dan snarled to the nearest man in uniform.

The officer glanced at Eric's face, and then his leg, and got on his radio.

"Oh, don't bother. He's a useless little shit who's been expelled—" Andreas stepped forward, right arm useless by his side. Blood leaked from his mouth, and Eric could see where several of his teeth were missing. His elbow shot must have been better than he'd thought.

"Did you shoot him?" The most senior-looking cop stepped into Andreas' space.

"Of course I did. There's nothing you can do about it. This is an internal Corvian matter—"

"Dr. Alawi is an American resident, and the shooting took place in Cambridge. You can sort it out with the embassy, on your way home, pal." The

239

cop wasn't gentle about turning Andreas around and slapping handcuffs on him. "You have the right to remain silent. I highly recommend you exercise that right." He frog-marched Andreas out of the house, reciting his Miranda rights the whole time.

The crowd outside cheered.

Now paramedics rushed in—or maybe it was a minute or two, Eric couldn't quite tell. Everything had narrowed to a painful haze by now. Part of him wanted to laugh it off. After all, it was just a leg; he had two and it wasn't even a major injury. It shouldn't even hurt this much. He should be able to hobble out of here, that was how it worked on television.

He couldn't put weight on the leg at all though, and he was losing a lot of blood. He didn't fight the paramedics when they came and put him onto the stretcher, applying a bandage to the leg that seemed to hurt more than the injury itself and covering him with a sheet.

Dan wanted to come with him, and Eric wanted him to come more than anything. He hated the thought of going to the hospital alone, but he had more important things on his mind right now.

"Ada," he said, squeezing Dan's hand before they took him out.

240

The ambulance trip was short, only three minutes, but Eric still didn't remember it. The next thing he clearly remembered was waking up later that evening in a private room in the hospital. His leg throbbed from within a splendid white cast, and he'd been dressed in the tackiest hospital johnny ever.

Dan sat in a chair beside him, holding his hand. A little smile played around his lips. "Are you really awake this time?"

"I suppose? Maybe?" He groaned and fumbled for the bed controls he knew had to be nearby. "Where is Ada?"

Dan chuckled. "She's with the Omars. Let me give you some water." He held out a cup and pushed a button Eric hadn't found yet, one that helped Eric sit up. "Ada's beside herself. I had to send her a picture to prove you're alive."

Eric groaned. "I'm sure it's a lovely picture too." He took the water. "This might be the best thing I've ever tasted."

"I'll bet." Dan looked down. "I'm sorry I wasn't there to stop him."

Eric blinked at him. "Dan, we agreed. Protecting Ada is the most important thing on either of our plates. We spoke about this."

"I know. But I still hate knowing he hurt you." Dan combed his fingers through Eric's hair.

"You did good though. You kicked his ass. He wanted to kill you. Still does, according to Gomes and Rourke."

"Of course he does." Eric closed his eyes. "I suppose he'll take his shot."

"Not from here, he won't." Dan set his jaw. "Your father wants to talk with you, but before you call him back, you should know Andreas is already on a plane back to Corvia. Parliament or whoever had an emergency session. He'll get a trial, but he'll never be able to bother you again."

Eric closed his eyes. "You don't think so?"

"No. I don't. For one thing, he showed himself to be enough of a trigger-happy loon that he won't be allowed back into the States. I think there are some other conversations you need to have to get more clarity—I mean, I'm happy to talk about it, but I'm not in a position to give much detail." He pulled over the little tray table all hospitals seemed to use.

Eric's tablet sat on top, blank and almost reflective. "You want me to video chat with Sebastian. Now, from here."

"He's actually pretty anxious right now. About you, which surprised me. He wants to hear from your own lips that you're okay."

"I don't suppose they'd be willing to dose me out of my mind with morphine first?"

242

They both knew Eric was joking. He would never be willing to speak to his father while high. He took a deep breath, picked up his tablet, and called his father's number.

Sebastian's face flickered onto the screen right away. "Eric. That . . . man . . . of yours told me you survived, but I couldn't believe it until I saw you with my own eyes."

Eric almost dropped the tablet. Sebastian's eyes were actually bloodshot. It could have been from a hangover, but that wouldn't explain the swelling around them. He looked downright old today. "I haven't spoken to the doctors yet, but it's just a leg wound. I'm sure I'll be right as rain soon enough. Thank you for your concern."

Sebastian managed a little bit of a smile. "I know it sounds absurd, coming from me. I tried to prepare you all for what the world was like, with the gossipmongers and the politicians. I did wrong by all of you children, and I have to admit it now." He glanced away at something off-screen, heaved a huge sigh, and then bowed his head.

"I've spoken with the authorities in the United States. They think Andreas may have murdered Selene as well. It's difficult to prove. He covered his tracks well. She surprised us all when she gave the baby to you." He sighed again. "What was he thinking?"

243

Eric closed his eyes for a second. It shouldn't be on him to soothe the father who'd never given a damn about him. Not ever, and certainly not from a hospital bed. "He was thinking about image, about position, and about control. Our siblings seem to be keeping the gossip magazines in business, and Andreas apparently believed that if he could provide the world with a 'proper' royal, he could justify our family's position—and our allowance from the treasury." Eric chuckled, but without humor.

Dan picked up for him, which was good because Eric wasn't sure he could go on. "He thought if he got to her young enough, he could mold Ada into the right shape. He tried to lure Eric back, thinking enough of the furor had died down about his departure from Corvia, but when it didn't work, he tried humiliation."

Sebastian looked away, face twisted into an expression of disgust. "He thought he could restore the reputation of Corvian royalty by airing a sex tape? I may not approve of your lifestyle, Eric, but I must admit you got all of the brains in the family." He shook his head. "Regardless. What are your plans now?"

Eric looked at Dan. He didn't dare bring up their future, not like this. Not in front of Sebastian, not while he lay here in a hospital bed.

244

Dan didn't seem to feel any such compunctions. "I think Eric and I need to sit down and discuss plans for Ada. Neither of us will make a decision without the other, and our niece is the most important factor in all of this. She depends on us for everything, including her actual safety."

Sebastian narrowed his eyes at Dan, and then he wiped his face. "Forgive me. I've been stuck in my old ways for too long. I'll admit I'd hoped Eric would come home and contribute to the line of succession, especially in light of current events. I know women are not of particular interest, but there are ways." He held up a hand. "But, in good faith, this is foolish. He has found a man whom he loves, who loves him and stands by him even when his own flesh and blood did not.

"I am old, gentlemen," he continued, a sad look in his ice-blue eyes. "Andreas has been removed from the line of succession, thanks to a specific act of Parliament. Hans was declared unfit years ago by reason of the fact that he can't stop filling his veins with whatever looks exciting at the moment. Selene is dead, and of course, by law girls, cannot inherit until the male heirs have died.

"You are the heir apparent, Eric."

The monitor connected to Eric skipped a beat.

"Your Majesty, I haven't even set foot in Corvia in over a decade. I haven't been *welcome* in Corvia in over a decade. I certainly can't inherit. I can't stop being gay, and I wouldn't if I could. Perhaps Johan?"

Sebastian shook his head. "The right person to lead this kingdom is probably the person who's been kept the furthest from this wretched family, if I'm being honest. I know you won't say yes yet. You'll want to talk it over. But I wanted you to know that as of right now, you are next in line for the Corvian throne.

"And I wanted you to know that I'm sorry, Eric. For everything."

The screen went blank.

Eric stared at Dan. Dan stared at Eric.

"Well, that was . . ." Dan took a deep breath. "I knew he wanted to apologize. I didn't know he was going to lay the rest of that shit on you."

Eric raised an eyebrow.

"What? You've got like fifty siblings, okay? How was I supposed to know?"

Eric laughed softly. "We should talk about this. But right now, I don't want to think about Corvia."

"You probably want the good stuff." Dan reached for the nurse call button.

Eric stopped him. "You are the good stuff, Dan."

Chapter Twenty-Two

Dan pinched himself underneath the ridiculous tuxedo the Protocol Droid—er, Official—insisted he had to wear for this shindig. He'd survived war, loss, and horrific attacks on the man he loved, and had come out with his mental health more or less intact. His and Eric's coronation as king and prince consort of Corvia was turning out to be the one thing that could possibly destroy his grasp of reality

So was the fact that they even had an actual royal official whose whole job it was to fuss over things like traditional outfits and meals.

Technically, they'd ascended to the throne a month ago, when Sebastian finally released his clawlike grasp on life. Plenty of Eric's half siblings had tried to outmaneuver their brother's return from the States, but a majority from both houses of Parliament had stopped them.

Even the religious bloc, a notoriously conservative group, who'd argued strenuously for Eric's exile at fifteen, preferred a gay scientist and attorney who was nominally Muslim to what the rest of the royal family had become. And none of them were at all interested in abolishing the monarchy entirely, much to Eric's dismay.

And so here they sat, on ancient wooden chairs painted gold by some complete doofus five centuries ago, with heavy metal crowns that weighed as much as an infant on each of their heads, holding hands in a formal posture while the Speaker of the Commons read out a long and boring speech in a language Dan barely understood. He'd been trying to learn German ever since he and Eric agreed they'd accept what life was giving them. Dan thought he was doing okay with it.

He wasn't doing well enough to follow this speech. Maybe it was the repetition of phrases like *restoring the glory of thy ancestors* that was turning his brain into tapioca.

And so many pictures. So many cameras. It wasn't just the paparazzi either. Respectable news organizations from around the world had sent reporters to cover the event, and if Dan had been at home in America, even he might have tuned in. It was, after all, an historic occasion. There had been gay kings before, but none of them, since the Roman emperors, had thought to crown their same-sex spouses at their sides.

Even that had been received with the sharp end of an axe.

The people of Corvia seemed to accept Eric and Dan with equanimity for the most part, and for tonight, no one seemed interested in upsetting the joyful mood of the occasion. Other crowned heads of state either attended or sent their own representatives. Dan had met them. He couldn't keep them straight. He didn't think he was expected to, the Protocol Droid's muttered comments notwithstanding.

Finally, the droning was over. Eric did some kind of a *thing*, with his hand, and Dan knew it was time to stand up. They rose to their feet, the crowd also rose, and everyone cheered. The Corvian national anthem played as they proceeded from the cathedral, followed by "The Star-Spangled Banner."

Dan hadn't known that was on the playlist. Eric stared straight ahead, but Dan could see the little grin on his face, and his heart swelled even larger.

There was a reception after the coronation, an exclusive affair to which Eric insisted a certain number of normal people from each of the electoral districts also be invited. A few of the old noblemen huffed and muttered about that, but Eric made sure he and Dan got to meet each and every one of them.

The Omars were there, of course. Eric had invited them, along with a handful of his favorite students. Dan was thrilled to see them because they'd been so helpful during the early days of his relationship with Eric, and they deserved to live it up a little.

So did Eric, to be honest.

Levi from Five Star was there too. So was Jamal King and his husband, the actor Owen Paul. Dan and Jamal were buddies and colleagues, and Dan figured it was only fair for him to have some of his friends here too. And of course, the camera just adored Owen, which kept it away from Dan and Eric when they needed a moment to themselves.

The reception didn't leave much time for deep conversations, just a few greetings here and there before the Coronation Banquet had to begin. This, too, had been a bone of contention. Apparently, the menu for the Coronation Banquet had been set when Saint Whoever had told King Whoever the First to establish a kingdom instead of a little gathering of tribes, and the thought of serving anything that didn't consist of eighty different forms of dead pig set traditional hearts afire.

While the new king was hardly observant, one of his few concessions to religion was in not consuming pork. He had no problem with other people eating it, but something else was going to need to be served to him and to his Muslim guests. And to his vegetarian guests.

While the Protocol Official recovered in the hospital, Hadiya quietly conferred with the royal chef, and they worked everything out between them. The archbishop of Corvia sniffed, and he complained, but after the Royal Banquet he privately admitted that some of the dishes on the official menu weren't to his liking anyway and he'd rather eat from "King Eric's menu."

Dan and Eric didn't get to go to bed until very late, although they did stop in to see Ada. Two years in the kingdom she'd avoided like plague had done wonders for her. Now six, she sat in the nursery with her cousin Sebastian, Andreas' son, their nanny Aisha, and Hadiya.

They'd all been watching the coverage on television.

Dan hadn't expected to like Andreas' son. Then he met him. The kid reminded him so much of Eric it wasn't even funny. He was too smart for his own good, but his mother hadn't been able to give him the academic advancement Eric had thanks to Andreas' control issues. Once he'd met Eric, he'd recognized a kindred soul, and Eric found him tutors and even sat with him to feed the boy's hungry mind.

He also quietly made arrangements to get Sebastian into some activities with boys his own age because he had enough self-awareness to know what had been missing from his own life.

If Sebastian understood he'd been excluded from the succession through no fault of his own, he didn't seem to mind. Maybe that would change eventually. He was only eight, after all. For now, he idolized his beloved uncles and followed them pretty much everywhere.

His mother had no objections to these changes at all. In fact, once Eric returned to Corvia, she filed for divorce and returned to Germany. "I still want to see Sebastian," she told Dan one evening, shortly before her departure. "I don't want to take him away from his country, and I don't want to lose him. But it's difficult too. His father was evil. His father was cruel, and I need some time to heal."

Dan patted her back and nodded. He couldn't think of much to add to that. "I think Eric's mother felt the same way."

"I can believe it." She glared back at the palace. "At least my Sebastian has Eric, and you. He's in good hands."

In the end, Sebastian went to Germany to see his mother on a quarterly basis. Seeing him here, standing up with Ada, Dan had to think they'd all won.

"Was it awful?" Ada tugged at Dan's sleeve, while Eric sat down in Sebastian's vacated spot. "Those hats didn't look very comfortable. Did they hurt? The speech was long. It looked boring. Was it boring? Who was the pretty guy the camera kept going back to? Do you have to do it again tomorrow? Can I have ice cream?"

Aisha shook her head, disapproving. "You've already had twice as much ice cream as you're supposed to have. You can have ice cream in the morning, it's time for bed now."

Dan shot her a grateful look before taking his niece's hand. "How about this. Eric and I will put you to bed, and you can help us to open Parliament tomorrow. Sound good?"

"Can I bang the hammer?" She gave Dan a cagey look.

"Parliament is boring." Sebastian yawned. "I'd rather play in the lab. Uncle Eric, can we look at those things you showed me? The ones that take the salt from water?"

255

Eric grinned and ruffled Sebastian's hair. "We absolutely can. I'll show you my latest design tomorrow. And it's okay if you'd rather do science than government. And it's just fine if Ada is more interested in government than science. As long as you both listen to each other and work together, it'll all work out fine."

Sebastian grinned and put an arm over Ada's shoulders. "There won't be a problem with that. We're best friends—aren't we, Ada?"

"We're like brother and sister!" Ada jumped up. "Come on, let's go, you can stay in my room and tell me about the solar panels again!"

Dan laughed and took Eric's hand as they tucked Ada and Sebastian in. Dan knew they'd stay up late talking about all the things they'd learned today. He should probably be concerned. He wasn't.

Now they could retreat to their own room and get rid of the stupid tuxedos. Dan still thought he should have been allowed to wear his dress uniform, but apparently, there were rules about that from the Army too. "I thought we'd never get those off." He climbed into bed, eschewing anything resembling clothing. "I'm still not sure the Protocol Droid isn't going to come in here and yell at me about my cufflinks or something."

256

Eric burst out laughing and slipped under the covers beside him. "Do you know, that man featured in my nightmares up until I was fifteen? I think he was old before my father was even born."

Dan snickered. "He was there when Saint Whatever dictated the first Coronation Banquet. It's why he had to go have a lie-down when you changed it." Then he sobered. "How are you doing? Are you okay?"

Eric paused. Then he looked up at Dan with big brown eyes. "How could I be anything but okay? I've got you?" He brushed his lips across Dan's. "It's not . . . anything like where I thought my life would be. But I never thought someone like you could be in it. What about you?"

"Are you kidding? I'm a little weirded out by some stuff. But you're right here by my side. As long as I've got you? I don't need anything else."

Also by J. V. Speyer

Hollywood Lighting (2020)
Smoked Gin (2020)
See Ya, Space Cowboy (2019)
Faith (2019)
Absolution (2019)
Hunter (2018)
Professional Courtesy (2018, MLR Books)
Snowed In: Ross and Ashton (2019, JMS Books)
Paper Hearts (2019, JMS Books)
Whirlwind (JMS Books, 2018)
Carriage House (NineStar Press, 2017)
The Dented Crown (2017)
Rites of Spring (Less Than Three, 2017)
Starlit (MLR Books, 2017)
Midnight (Less Than Three, 2016)

About the Author

J. V. Speyer has lived in upstate New York and rural Catalonia before making the greater Boston, Massachusetts, area her permanent home. She has worked in archaeology, security, accountancy, finance, and nonprofit management. She currently lives just south of Boston in a house old enough to remember when her town was a tavern community with a farming problem.

J. V. finds most of her inspiration from music. Her tastes run the gamut from traditional to industrial and back again. When not writing, she can usually be found enjoying a baseball game or avoiding direct sunlight. She's learning to crochet so she can make blankets to fortify herself against the cold.

J. V. can be found on Twitter or Instagram at @JVSpeyer, or on Facebook at https://www.facebook.com/JVSpeyerAuthor. You can get exclusive updates, cocktail recipes, and other notes here: http://eepurl.com/dtlwBH

www.ingramcontent.com/pod-product-compliance
Lightning Source LLC
Chambersburg PA
CBHW061954170626
46813CB00006B/2635